Hi, I'm JIMMY!

Like me, you probably noticed the world is run by adults.

But ask yourself: Who would do the best job
of making books that *kids* will love?

Yeah. **Kids!**

So that's how the idea of JIMMY books came to life.

We want every JIMMY book to be so good that when you're finished,
you'll say,

"PLEASE GIVE ME ANOTHER BOOK!"

Give this one a try and see if you agree.
(If not, you're probably an adult!)

JIMMY PATTERSON BOOKS FOR YOUNG READERS

For exclusives, trailers, and other information, visit jimmypatterson.org.

JAMES PATTERSON
AND CHRIS GRABENSTEIN
ILLUSTRATED BY KERASCOËT

Jimmy Patterson Books
Little, Brown and Company
New York Boston London

Copyright © 2017 by James Patterson
Illustrations by Kerascoët

JIMMY Patterson Books / Little, Brown and Company
Hachette Book Group
1290 Avenue of the Americas, New York, NY 10104
JimmyPatterson.org

First Paperback Edition: September 2017
Originally published in hardcover by Little, Brown and Company, March 2016

JIMMY Patterson Books is an imprint of Little, Brown and Company, a division of Hachette Book Group, Inc. The Little, Brown name and logo are trademarks of Hachette Book Group, Inc. The JIMMY Patterson Books™ name and logo are trademarks of JBP Business, LLC.

The publisher is not responsible for websites (or their content) that are not owned by the publisher.

The Hachette Speakers Bureau provides a wide range of authors for speaking events. To find out more, go to hachettespeakersbureau.com or call (866) 376-6591.

Dialogue and lyrics from *You're a Good Man, Charlie Brown* by Clark Gesner.
Based on the comic strip *Peanuts* by Charles M. Schulz.
Dialogue copyright © 1967 by Clark Gesner.
Lyrics copyright © 1971 by Jeremy Music, Inc.

Library of Congress Cataloging-in-Publication Data

Patterson, James

Jacky Ha-Ha / James Patterson and Chris Grabenstein ;
illustrated by Kerascoët. — First edition.
pages cm
Summary: "Twelve-year-old Jacky 'Ha-Ha' Hart is a class clown with a penchant for pranking—and when she's required to act in the school play to appease her frustrated teachers, she must conquer her stutter"— Provided by publisher.

ISBN 978-0-316-26249-1 (hardcover) — ISBN 978-0-316-43253-5 (paperback)—
ISBN 978-0-316-30302-6 (ebook) — ISBN 978-0-316-30300-2 (library edition ebook)
[1. Behavior—Fiction. 2. Practical jokes—Fiction. 3. Stuttering—Fiction. 4. Theater—Fiction. 5. Middle schools—Fiction. 6. Schools—Fiction. 7. Family life—Fiction. 8. Humorous stories.] I. Grabenstein, Chris, author. II. Kerascoët. III. Title.
PZ7.P27653Jac 2016
[Fic]—dc23
2015007626

10 9 8 7 6 5 4 3 2 1

LSC-H

Printed in the United States of America

For Schaak Van Deusen,
my first drama coach
and favorite English teacher.
—CG

For my mom,
my favorite English teacher.
—JP

PROLOGUE

For my Darling Daughters
Tina & Grace

Yes, girls, this might just be the biggest night of my life and I'm sitting here doodling.

But doodling is what I always do when I get nervous, and I don't think I'll ever be more nervous than I am right *now* because I'm about to hop into a limousine and head off to the Academy Awards, where I could maybe, just maybe, win an Oscar!

Can you girls believe this? Your very own mom

is one of only five nominees for Best Actress! Okay, it wasn't a huge stretch to play a dirt-poor street performer in Atlantic City, but it's not often that a *comedy* gets any awards.

What's even rarer is when funny girls win the Oscar for Best Actress. I think the last time was 1977, when Diane Keaton won for *Annie Hall*.

I wasn't even born in 1977. That means you guys weren't, either.

Anyway, there's a twenty percent chance that I might have to give a sp-sp-sp-speech tonight in front of m-m-m-millions of people, which, as you might imagine, terrifies me beyond my ability to put terror into w-w-w-words.

If, by some miracle, I actually do win the Best Actress Oscar for *Cracking Up,* the first thing I'm going to do, of course, is thank you two for making me laugh every day since you were born. Unless I trip on my gown. If *that* happens, the first thing I'm going to do is stand back up and adjust stuff.

Uh-oh, my purse is shaking! Either Los Angeles is having another one of its famous earthquakes or my producers are texting me to say it's time to go.

Before I do…

There's something else I want to tell you guys.

After we finished filming *Cracking Up,* and before I went back to work at *Saturday Night Live,* I wrote a book. *This* book.

It's all about when I was a kid.

That's right. Once upon a time, I was actually your age. Before that, I was even younger. It's true. I have, in my past, been both an infant and a toddler.

The story I want to tell you guys took place when I was twelve. It starts when I decided to climb up to the top of the Ferris wheel on the Seaside Heights boardwalk in New Jersey. It was after midnight, so the ride was locked up tight. But that didn't stop me. I was a girl on a mission.

You could say I was a little crazy back in the 1990s. (Heck, we all were. We danced to music by two guys named Milli Vanilli.)

It wasn't just that I wanted to have a look out over the Atlantic Ocean. I was also wondering what I'd be like when I grew up, *if* I grew up. Maybe I had convinced myself that by scaling the Ferris wheel and staring out at the ocean, I might be able to see my future, somewhere off on the horizon.

Did I mention I was a little crazy back then?

I did my best to tell the story of that wild year at the shore just the way it really was for me, warts and all—though at twelve years old, it was more like *pimples* and all—because I think there's a tendency for parents not to tell the whole truth about how it was for them growing up.

So here it is, ladies—the funny, the not-so funny, and the embarrassingly true.

CHAPTER 1

O kay, let me set the scene.

It's the absolutely worst day of any year ever recorded since history has been recorded. That, of course, would be the last day of summer vacation. The day before school starts.

The year is 1990. President Bush (the first one, George *H. W.*) tells the world he doesn't like broccoli and hasn't liked it since he was a little kid, when his mother made him eat it. Donkey Kong is about as good as it gets in video games. And guys are wearing mullets. They're about as hideous as a hairstyle can be—short at the front and sides, long in the back. Kind of like a coonskin cap made out of hair.

Mullet
↓
BLINK!

I'm living with my six sisters (your aunts) in a tiny house near the beach in Seaside Heights. Think Little Women living on the Jersey Shore, but none of us have questionable names like Snooki or JWoww.

Our father is pretty strict. He makes sure we keep our little house spick-and-span and "shipshape," even though it's a bungalow, not a boat.

We have to do *all* of our chores before we can do anything remotely fun—even though it's the last day of summer.

"Put some elbow grease into it, girls!" That's Emma. She's only six, but she does an awesome Dad impression.

We all call Emma the Little Boss. She's incredibly stubborn, but fortunately for her, also incredibly cute.

The rest of us gab up a storm while we wash windows, beat rugs, clean up the kitchen, and scrub the toilets. Remember, this was before texting. In 1990, we actually *talked* to each other. Weird, right?

My oldest sister, Sydney, who was nineteen that year, isn't home right now because her summer ended early. She went off to college (Princeton), where she is a freshman. (Ever wonder why colleges don't have freshwomen? Are they all stale? That's the kind of goofy thing I think about sometimes.)

As you might imagine, Sydney is adored by the whole family, parents and grandparents included. She is practically perfect in every possible way.

That means she's the exact opposite of me.

CHAPTER 2

Being born a girl in the middle of a pack of girls makes me about as special as a brown M&M. I'm fourth in line to the throne, which, in our house, would be the toilet I have to scrub with stinky blue chemicals before I can go outside and have some end-of-summer fun. And with seven people sharing our single bathroom, it's no quick thing to get it clean.

I guess you could say I'm something of a tomboy. While all the other girls on the Seaside Heights beach are wearing bright red *Baywatch* one-piece swim-suits or teeny-weeny bikinis, I prefer cut-off blue

jeans and my baggiest New York Giants T-shirt.
I also have a very funny sun hat. Okay, it's a sombrero.

The only sister younger than me (besides Emma,
the Little Boss, of course) is Riley. She's eleven.

I feel sorry for Riley. She's in the very unfortunate position of having me as her big sister.

You see, the problem is, Riley looks up to me. She's my sidekick and partner in crime, not that we've ever done anything that's actually, you know, criminal. Okay, some of the pranks we pull are borderline illegal, but I think a halfway-decent lawyer could easily get us out of jail free (my favorite card in Monopoly). Riley is always skating on the edge of the abyss because that's where I like to hang out. In the danger zone.

You'll see.

My parents' other middle child is Hannah.

Hannah is fourteen and too nice for words. She's so sweet they won't let her into the candy stores on the boardwalk anymore because they're afraid of the competition. Also because she likes to help herself to samples of peanut butter fudge. Every day. For hours at a time.

Hannah has a huge crush on Mike Guadagno, a rich kid from Stonewall Prep. It's kind of sad and, also, kind of funny.

My sister Victoria (don't you dare call her Vickie) is fifteen going on fifty.

Victoria has advice about everything for everyone, and she *loves* to share it with you, any time of the day or night. She's a bookworm, a movie nut, and a library nerd. She also keeps a diary and likes to inform you when she intends to write about something you just did. Victoria never shuts up, not even in her sleep. One night, I'm sure I heard her giving advice to the monster in her nightmare on how to scare her better.

Finally, there's Sophia, the second oldest—or, as she likes to say, *the* oldest because Sydney is off at college.

Sophia is eighteen and in love (temporarily) with Mike Guadagno.

That's right. The same rich kid from Stonewall

Prep that Hannah has a crush on, hence the sad-funny thing I was talking about earlier. Sophia doesn't know about Hannah's feelings for Mike. Mike doesn't, either. (Victoria does and has advised against them. Repeatedly.)

Mike Guadagno is a nice guy, actually. He's what Mom would call a keeper, which means, basically, he's a fish you wouldn't toss back into the ocean after you hauled it into your boat and ripped the hook out of its mouth. I sort of feel sorry for Mike. We all do. As soon as summer's over, we know Sophia is going to rip out her hook and break Mike's heart. It's her thing. She collects boys the way a botanist collects flowers or a bugologist collects beetles.

My new friend Meredith Crawford, who recently moved to Seaside Heights from Newark, tells me there's no such thing as a bugologist when I tell her about Sophia and how she plays "impossible to get."

"Scientists who study insects are called entomologists," she says.

Meredith is super-smart. I'm hoping she'll help me do my homework when school starts. She already pitches in with the chores around our house because

she practically lives at our place and we need all the help we can get.

My mom (your grandmother) doesn't do much housekeeping. No cooking, no cleaning. Nothing.

She can't.

She's in Saudi Arabia.

CHAPTER 3

Another thing that happened in 1990?

A crazy dictator with a bushy mustache named Saddam Hussein (the crazy guy, not the bushy mustache) invaded Kuwait because he thought they were charging too much for gas.

Hey, I don't like the price the guy on the corner charges, but do you see me invading his gas station?

Anyway, after Saddam refused to remove his troops from Kuwait, President George H. W. Bush (the guy who hates broccoli) ordered the start of Operation Desert Shield.

Mom, who everybody calls Big Sydney—not because she's large or anything but because she came before Little Sydney, my oldest sister—is a staff sergeant in the Marine Corps. The second that President Bush declared Operation Desert Shield, Mom had to pack up her gear and ship out for Saudi Arabia, where America's troops were stationed, waiting for Saddam to do the right thing, which would be to leave Kuwait without breaking anything.

MOM
with some of her pals heading off to the Persian Gulf

That's why we Hart girls are on double cleaning duty these days. We're in charge of everything in our small house, from basically raising Emma (and sometimes Riley) to checking in on Mom's mom (our grandmother Nonna) and walking Sandfleas. She's our dog.

I flush the toilet and watch the blue foamy water swirl away. My final chore is finished.

"Let's book!" I say to my friend Meredith. (Quick translation: "Let's book" in the 1990s means "Let's get outta here," not "Shall we read something by Dr. Seuss?")

"What do you want to do?" I ask, hoping she has an incredible idea that would be the perfect end to our summer vacation.

"I don't know. What do *you* want to do?"

I'm about to say "I don't know" when I have my best end-of-the-summer brainstorm *ever*.

"Let's hit the boardwalk and play a new game," I say to Meredith.

Riley asks if she can tag along.

"We might do something stupid," I warn her.

Riley shrugs. "Stupid is cool."

She'll regret that decision later, trust me.

CHAPTER 4

We walk two blocks east to the boardwalk. The instant we're up the steps, the smell of sizzling Italian sausage sandwiches slathered with grilled onions and limp green peppers attacks my nostrils. I lay out the rules of my new game.

"We have to eat every single type of food there is on the boardwalk."

"Huh?" says Meredith.

"Curly fries, zeppoles, orange-and-white swirl cones, deep-fried Oreos, pizza, Philly cheesesteaks…"

"We'll get sick," says Riley.

"Maybe," I say. "But whoever eats the most is the winner!"

"What do they win?"

"An amazing prize," I tell Riley. "No chores. For

the whole month of September! No dishes, no mopping, no toilet scrubbing."

"I'm in," says Meredith enthusiastically, which is a little silly because she doesn't have to do any chores in our house *anyway*.

"Me too," says Riley.

And so it begins. First stop—funnel cakes!

The three of us giggle as we gobble up paper plates full of squiggly fried dough dusted with powdered sugar.

Then we move down the boardwalk to devour hot dogs and pepperoni pizza slices and big, salty pretzels. We slosh down all of that bready gunk with Kohr's fresh fruit orangeade, which I don't think has any fruit at all in it, unless sugar counts.

Poor Riley drops out when we move on to Philly cheesesteaks—sandwiches dripping with some kind of white, cheeselike goo, onions, and gobs of fatty meat.

After Meredith and I munch our meat bombs, we move on to Dippin' Dots, which have been called the future of ice cream for like thirty years and, still, the only place I ever see the frozen pebbles is on the Jersey Shore boardwalk.

"Maybe astronauts will eat them when we colonize Mars," I say, which reminds Meredith that we haven't eaten a deep-fried candy bar yet, so we find a food stand that serves them.

In fact, we both wolf down three batter-dipped, deep-fried Baby Ruth bars. And some deep-fried Ring Dings. And some deeper-fried curly fries.

This is when our stunt gets truly awesome—we're starting to attract a crowd. A real, live audience!

I'm in heaven!

CHAPTER 5

Yes, there's nothing better than a mob of perfect strangers paying attention to you, especially when you're a middle child who's semi-invisible at home.

Now that Mom's off with her marine unit in the Persian Gulf, I lost fifty percent of any parental attention I could get, which isn't much with six sisters. Dad has to work all day. He's tired when he gets home. He has bills to pay and a car to take care of and a gaggle of girls driving him goofy. We're lucky if he can remember all of our names. He doesn't have time to actually pay attention to us one-on-one.

A guy in our audience hands us a white bakery bag.

"Two elephant ears," he says. "One for each of youse."

Elephant ears are these gigantic, flaky cookies the size of, well, elephant ears.

I'm chomping away, nibbling my way around the circle (which, incidentally, is the only way you could eat something the size of a manhole cover), but I'm slowing down some. My stomach has ballooned out to the size of a beach ball. Meanwhile, our crowd has swollen to dozens of people, maybe as many as fifty! Our eat-a-thon is a huge hit and I'm feeling great.

Until I don't.

"You had any of these yet, girls?" A devil in a Hawaiian shirt offers us a platter of greasy, lumpy, cheesy chili nachos.

The nachos resemble a pile of steaming dog poop

on a pile of tortilla chips, and just looking at it gets my gag reflex going. Meredith's, too.

"I think I might regurgitate," she mumbles.

(See, I told you she was smarter than me.)

All I come up with is "I'm going to blow chunks!"

And the two of us toss our cookies. And our pizza. And our deep-fried Baby Ruth bars. And everything else we ate in the last two hours. We're spewing brown chunky junk like a pair of berserk sewer pipes. I totally ruin my sombrero, which I'd thought would make a good vomit bucket.

Why do I do these things to myself? I wonder as I watch the food I ate make a repeat appearance. *Why?*

It's a question I ask a lot.

(*Why do I let Jacky Hart do these things to me?* is what Meredith asks herself.)

When we're finally done, I can't resist cracking a joke.

"Yum! More room for dessert. Fudge, anyone?"

At that, Meredith horfs up some more pavement pizza.

CHAPTER 6

Then things get worse. Much worse.

First, our audience disappears. Fast. I don't think they enjoyed our big, boffo, barfy finish.

"Come back tomorrow, folks!" I say as they walk away. "We're here all week."

"No, we're not," says Meredith. "Tomorrow's school, remember?"

Yes, I do. But I'd been trying to forget.

"Uh-oh," says Riley.

She sees something flashing in the sun, maybe a hundred yards up the boardwalk. She points and I see it, too.

It's silver. It's bouncing up and down. And it's coming closer.

"It's his whistle," wheezes Riley. "It's *Dad.*"

Our father, Mac Hart, wears a shiny silver whistle around his neck because he is the captain of the Seaside Heights Beach Patrol. That means he's the head lifeguard, which, of course, also means he's a total hunk.

There's a TV show in the '90s called *Baywatch* about a bunch of really good-looking lifeguards who love to run up and down the beach. But they only *wish* they could look as good as Captain Mac Hart. Even though he's not getting any younger, everyone says he's *still* the best-looking boy on the beach. Seriously. When they were dating, Mom had a special T-shirt made with BEST-LOOKING BOY ON THE BEACH printed across the chest in cartoony letters. Dad still wears it sometimes when he cleans out the gutters and stuff.

Once upon a time, Mac Hart left New Jersey and went to the University of South Carolina on a baseball scholarship.

He was even drafted by the New York Yankees. Okay, he played for the Oneonta Yankees in Oneonta, New York, but still, it was *the Yankees* and, technically, they were in New York State. Plus, lots of big baseball stars came out of the Oneonta minor-league team over the years: Don Mattingly, Bernie Williams, Jorge Posada. But not Mac Hart. Instead, he met Big Sydney, got married, put away his glove and cleats, had seven kids, and became a professional lifeguard down the shore in Seaside Heights, New Jersey.

I wish I could've seen him play.

"What happened?" Dad asks when he looks down and sees my soggy beach hat filled to the brim with a pool of semidigested junk food.

"W-w-we ate too much?" I say.

"And whose idea was that?"

I raise my hand. "M-m-mine." I've always been a prankster, but never a liar.

Dad just shakes his head. I am a major-league disappointment.

"Come on, girls. I'm driving you home."

"That's okay," I say, stifling a burp because, believe it or not, my stomach is still sort of full. "I'd rather w-w-walk."

"Young lady," says my father, whipping off his very dark sunglasses so I can see that he is scowling at me. "You're in no condition to walk."

"I'm fine," I say.

"No, Jacqueline, you are not. You're coming with me."

Yes, all of a sudden, I have my father's undivided attention and I wish I didn't.

"See you at home!" I say as cheerily as I can while patting my tummy. "The w-w-walk will do me good."

I turn tail and take off running like a marathoner.

"Jacky!" Dad hollers. "Stop! Stop this instant!"

I don't stop. I keep running.

Dad starts blowing his whistle.

And I start blowing chunks. While I run.

Never a good idea, guys. You sort of run through your very own smelly Technicolor rainbow.

Which is why I never wore that New York Giants T-shirt again, either.

CHAPTER 7

And that brings us to me climbing the Ferris wheel in Seaside Heights, because I don't think either of you wants to hear that I spent the rest of my last day of summer sitting in my room thinking about what I did, which is what my father told me to do.

Actually, the whole sitting-in-your-room thing isn't that bad if you have books, which I did. Especially funny, spoofy, snarky books like *Mad About Town* and *Fighting Mad,* written by the "usual gang of idiots" who also write *Mad* magazine.

Around midnight, when everybody else is asleep,

I crawl out my bedroom window. Good thing it's on the first floor...it makes sneaking out much easier. I wind up with fewer broken bones.

By the way, what I'm doing is extremely dangerous. No one in their *right* mind would, should, or could really do this. But I promised you I'd tell you the truth, so here I go.

First, I have to weave my way through all the sketchy characters and rowdy college kids bumbling around in the shadows of Seaside Heights after midnight.

And then...I have to climb a Ferris wheel.

Don't try this at home, kids. Or at the county fair. Or Disney World. Or anywhere there might be a huge wheel made out of steel.

The Ferris wheel in Seaside Heights is on the Funtown Pier, which juts out over the Atlantic Ocean. I creep up on it from the beach, which means my sneakers will be full of sand when I start climbing. I probably should've worn socks.

In the daylight, you can tell the gondola cars are painted red, white, and blue. Very patriotic. At night, they just look like gray, kind of gray, and darker gray.

The first half of the climb is actually pretty easy. I ladder up the nicely spaced struts on the support beams that form a triangle to anchor the wheel's giant axle.

To get to the top, however, I have to hoist myself, monkey-bar style, up the slanted supports between crossbeams like I'm climbing a very slippery rope.

Once more, I'll remind you that I was crazy when I was twelve.

And fearless.

With one last *"mmph,"* I swing around and sort of straddle the edge of the wheel and just sit there, staring out at the ocean and the twinkling sky.

It's beautiful. Almost worth the trip.

I look for signs of my future out on the horizon. It's kind of dark. Hopefully that's because it's one o'clock in the morning and not because my future is extremely grim.

I take in a deep breath, and with the stars and the ocean and God as my witness, I make a solemn vow.

"I am doing this insane thing tonight," I say to who- or whatever is listening, "because tomorrow, I'm going to start a *sane* year at school. My first noncrazy year ever. I'm going to fulfill my 'tremendous potential,' the one my teachers are always telling me I'm wasting. I'm going to stop being the class clown, smart aleck, and wisenheimer. I'm also going to write more letters to Mom over in Saudi Arabia, visit Nonna in her nursing home more often, and be nicer to Dad and my sisters, especially Riley.

"I also solemnly swear that, this year, I will do a lot of other things I can't think of right now because I'm perched precariously at the top of this

Ferris wheel and the steel is pinching my thighs, which makes it incredibly difficult to think of stuff to solemnly swear about. But you'll see...I'm going to be a new me. No more Jacky Ha-Ha! This I do solemnly swear, amen."

To punctuate my promise, I raise my right hand and start howling at the moon.

I mean I'm really *AH-WOO*ing like the Wolf Man.

Even though I just promised I would stop doing funny stuff, I figure the howling is my last big hurrah.

As for the name Jacky Ha-Ha? We'll get to that in a minute.

First, I have to climb down from the darn Ferris wheel.

CHAPTER 8

Here's another confession: That particular nickname has been with me since pre-K.

I had a really bad stutter back then. In 1990, I'm more of a stammerer, except when I'm embarrassed or excited or p-p-panicked. Yes, this is why I've hated making speeches my whole life. And why I wasn't too crazy about chatting with my dad on the boardwalk after I'd eaten one of everything, especially with Meredith and Riley watching.

In pre-K, the other kids would ask me what my name was and I'd sputter out "Jacky Ha-Ha-Ha-Ha-Ha-Hart!" They'd laugh so hard, milk and Oreo pieces would come shooting out of their noses.

I didn't like that. And not just because they were squirting me with soggy cookie crumbs.

Nope, I didn't like it because those kids were laughing *at* me, not *with* me. I needed to turn that around.

So, when I was eight and working my way through elementary school, I took on the role of the class clown. I'd make funny faces, crack smart remarks, and repeat a lot of knock-knock jokes, which, with me, were always kn-kn-kn-knock, kn-kn-kn-knock jokes. The other kids loved them. Especially the way I could make the knock-knock bit last so long and sound so silly.

In third grade, on a particularly good April Fools' Day, I got away with murder by saying "April Fools!" after every funny thing I said about the teacher's hair and wardrobe choices. After that epic day, Jacky Ha-Ha-Ha-Hart officially became Jacky Ha-Ha, queen of comedy. Princess of pranks. Wizard of wisecracks.

You get the idea.

All my classmates love it when I say something dumb or crack a joke. I'm also pretty famous for my pranks. For instance, one day, back in fifth grade, we heard we were getting a substitute teacher. Before she came into the classroom, I told everybody to switch seats but answer "Here" when the sub called out the name of the kid who was supposed to be sitting in their seat. Roll call was a riot. The substitute teacher probably still thinks my name is Lori Dobbins.

I can also do an awesome droplet sound. You know—that noise you make by puckering up your lips and flicking your cheek so it sounds like there is a leak drip-drip-dripping somewhere in the room.

Once, during a math pop quiz, I did enough droplets for the teacher to call off the test while the janitor searched inside the ceiling for a toxic chemical spill.

Yep, being Jacky Ha-Ha has made me pretty popular at school (well, not with the janitors). Sure, it's also landed me in the assistant principal's office and the detention hall from time to time, but such is the price you pay for fame.

But this is the year I'm going to lose the *Ha-Ha* from my name and just be regular old Jacky Hart.

After all, I did make a solemn vow at the top of the Ferris wheel with all the angels in heaven listening. That should be enough to make me keep my promise.

Right?

CHAPTER 9

It's the first day of school, and I should've worn my I'M ALLERGIC TO ALGEBRA T-shirt, because the instant Mr. Wymer starts in with the *x*s and the *y*s, all I can think is *Algebra...WHY?*

And once I think it, it only takes a microsecond for the thought to reach my lips, too fast for me to stop it—vow or no vow.

"Why, oh, why, do we need *x* and *y?*"

The class cracks up. Even Mr. Wymer smiles. (Teachers are usually pretty cool if, as the class clown, your jokes are semiwitty.)

By the way, I'm pretty good at math. Have been my whole life. I just didn't get the point of it back then.

"Factoring for y," Mr. Wymer explains, trying to turn my smart-aleck remark into a teachable moment, "helps us find x."

Here's where I should have remembered those angels in heaven and the extremely serious promise I made to them, and sat back down. Instead, I say, "I can find x without y."

"Really? And how do you find x without knowing the value of y in this equation, Miss Hart?" He picks up a chunk of chalk and writes "$x + y = 25$."

"Simple," I say, gesturing at the blackboard. "X is the first letter you wrote down. See? I found it."

Two dozen twelve-year-olds howl with laughter.

Mr. Wymer's ears turn bright red. He's no longer smiling.

"Very amusing, Jacky. Now, if you don't mind, I'd like to continue teaching math to those students who came to class hoping to learn something besides just how funny you are."

He gives me a look. It's not a pretty one.

It also makes me stutter.

"Y-y-yes, sir."

I *hate* when that happens.

So, for the rest of the period, I plot my revenge.

I'm thinking about going with the birdseed-in-the-parking-lot bit. You know, I buy a sack of bird feed and sprinkle it on Mr. Wymer's car first thing in the morning. When he's ready to drive home in the afternoon, his car is fully decorated with a ton of white gunk left behind by all the birdies who dropped by for the all-you-can-eat buffet.

"Miss Hart?"

My scheming is interrupted when, with only two minutes left in the period, Mr. Wymer calls me up to the blackboard and hands me a stubby piece of chalk. While I was daydreaming about birdseed, he'd been drawing lines on the board.

"Name a pair of vertical angles," says Mr. Wymer.

I stare at the lines.

NOTHING IN HERE...

ScRitch
ScRitch

Mr. Wymer is smirking. He knows I haven't been paying attention for at least fifteen minutes.

I hear a titter rising up behind me.

The math class is taking me back to my pre-K days. The awful memory of kids laughing *at* me starts replaying in my head.

I put an end to that fast by scribbling on the board.

"There you go, Mr. Wymer," I say, stepping away to reveal my masterpiece. "I named two of 'em."

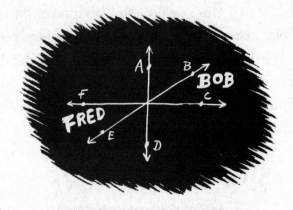

While the class is hooting, I tap the C.

"I was going to name this line Mr. Pointy, but you said you only needed two names. By the way, I also know why you can't ever find *your* 'ex.' She left. And I know why. Algebra's boring."

My classmates erupt in howling laughter as the

bell rings. The first day of my new school year is over.

I try my best to blend in with my audience as they stream out of the room.

"Not so fast, Miss Hart," says Mr. Wymer.

He reaches for the pink pad on his desk.

I know that pink pad.

It means I've just earned my first detention for the new school year.

Jeez, I was so close. I almost made it to the bell.

Mr. Wymer hands me my punishment. "Please go to the assistant principal's office to see Mrs. Turner."

"But school's over...."

He shakes his head. "Not for you, Jacky."

He doesn't add the *Ha-Ha,* but I hear it anyway. One day of school, and I've already blown my solemn vow.

CHAPTER 10

*F*ive detentions for one joke?

I can't believe it. What a total overreaction.

I take the pink slip to the assistant principal's office.

"Ah, Miss Hart," says Mrs. Turner. "We're right back where we left off last June. You, darkening my doorway with yet another pink slip of paper."

She reaches out and flicks her fingers in a "gimme" gesture.

I turn in my detention notice. She looks at it and makes like she's impressed.

"Wow. Five big ones? On the first day of school? What'd you do—make fun of Mr. Wymer's divorce?"

they should engrave my name on it.

Okay, I need to say something here.

When I cracked that joke about Mr. Wymer and his "ex," I did not realize that he had just spent his summer vacation going through an ugly divorce from a wife who thought he was boring because all he wanted to do with his life was teach kids like me how to solve math problems.

This is one of the major drawbacks of being quick-witted. You seldom give yourself enough time to fully consider the consequences before you open your mouth and say something hysterically clever (and totally offensive).

"Dumb move, Jacky," says Mrs. Turner. "And you're a smart girl. Or you could be."

Yes, Mrs. Turner is one of those grown-ups who always tell me I'm wasting my "tremendous potential."

"It was just a joke," I say. "Jokes are not five-detention crimes."

"True," says Mrs. Turner. "You usually have to punch somebody to get five. Or start a food fight in the cafeteria. That's a fiver for sure...."

"I didn't hurt anybody."

"Actually, Jacky, this time you did."

"Not on purpose."

"Doesn't matter what your intentions were."

I slump down in a chair. "This is so unfair."

"Yeah," says Mrs. Turner. "Kind of reminds me of life. And here's the kicker, Jacky: You're way ahead of the curve. You've got five big ones and we don't even start detention hall until next week because all of my teachers are too busy setting up their classrooms and putting together lesson plans to babysit our bad apples."

"I'm not a b-b-bad apple."

Mrs. Turner props her elbows on her desk. Drills her eyes into mine.

We're about to get serious here, folks.

"Look, Jacky," she says. "You're a very bright, very funny young girl. I know how hard it is for you when your mom's away...serving our country..."

How would she know how hard it is? It's not like she—or anyone—ever asked.

But all I do is stammer. "We're doing f-f-fine."

"I'm glad to hear it. But, Jacky, I cannot have you constantly disrupting classes."

"I'll do better. I promise."

"You've promised before."

I take a deep breath. "This time I made a vow."

"Really?"

"Yeah. Last night."

"Good. Well, I want to help you keep that vow." She pulls a thin book out of her top desk drawer. "Over the summer, we hired a new teacher for Honors English."

Honors English? That means I'll never meet her.

"Her name is Ms. O'Mara. She's also going to run our drama club. I think you should be in the fall production."

Mrs. Turner slides the book across the desk.

I read the title of the play: *You're A Good Man, Charlie Brown.*

"It's based on the comic strip," explains Mrs. Turner.

"Yeah," I say. "I figured. Hey, do you ever think Snoopy looks dead when he's snoozing on top of his doghouse?" Once I start, I can't stop. I go on a nervous ramble. "And what's with Charlie Brown? The guy only has one shirt. Does he even own a pair of pants? I mean, it looks like he's always wearing shorts...or a dress...."

My weak jokes don't sidetrack Mrs. Turner. "You have so much creative energy, Jacky," she says. "Being in the school play would be an excellent way to channel it into something productive. I'm told Ms. O'Mara knows a lot about theater. Apparently, she was a child star on Broadway."

"And now she's a schoolteacher in New Jersey. So much for being a star."

"Jacky? I'll make this simple. You have a choice.

58

You can try out for the school play, and if you get in, we'll forget about this pink slip and you can spend your after-school hours going to rehearsal. Or you can waste those same hours sitting in detention hall. Think about it. Talk it over with your dad."

"That's okay, I d-d-don't really—"

"He's waiting for you at his office. I told him you'd be dropping by. Don't keep him waiting."

Mrs. Turner gestures toward the door.

I glance down at the Charlie Brown script.

It's a musical.

Jacky Ha-Ha doesn't sing. Especially not in p-p-public.

CHAPTER 11

I stomp out of school, muttering under my breath.

I cannot believe this onslaught of overreactions.

Five detentions for a stupid joke?

Wanting to shove me onstage in the school play where anybody who buys a ticket can laugh at me as I stumble and stutter my way through my l-l-lines and s-s-songs?

And now I have to go see Dad down at his "office" (which is what he calls the beach), where he's sitting high up on his lifeguard chair, waiting to whip off his sunglasses and glare down at me?

Well, actually, maybe I'll take that as a positive.

If my father is glaring at me, at least he's, momentarily, paying attention to me.

Since the summer is over, Dad's "office" is nearly deserted. He's in his lifeguard stand, staring out at the ocean, being disappointed in me.

Jenny Cornwall is up there with him.

Remember how my mom said my dad was the best-looking boy on the beach? Well, that's what everybody says about Jenny Cornwall. Not that she's a boy. That she's the "prettiest girl on the beach."

Jenny Cornwall used to be a cop down in Trenton, but she got shot and decided lifeguarding was a safer bet. You can still see the scar from the bullet wound on the side of her thigh since her bathing suit shows off a lot of skin, especially in the hip and thigh department. A lot of *tan* skin.

The instant I enter Dad's peripheral vision (lifeguards have the best peripheral vision in the world,

by the way), he tips up his shades and says, without even looking at me, "Five detentions on the first day of school? Tell me this isn't true."

I look down at my feet. "It's true."

I can see Jenny Cornwall's shadow slanting across the sand. She's shaking her head. Yes, even the prettiest girl on the beach is disappointed with me.

"What's your mother going to say when I tell her about this?" asks Dad.

I look up. "Do you have to tell her?"

"Of course I do. We're your parents. Plus, she might have some ideas about what to do with you, because, frankly, I'm all out of them, Jacky."

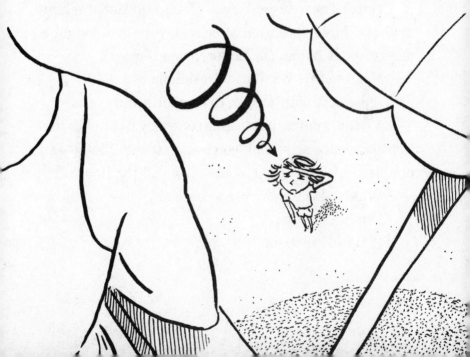

"Why do you have to be this way?" he continues. "Why can't you buckle down and be more like Victoria? Life isn't a joke, Jacky. Nobody gets to laugh all the time. Do you seriously think there's anything funny about paying a mortgage and putting food on the table?"

"If it was serious, it couldn't be funny," I say.

"What?"

"You asked me if I seriously thought it was funny…"

"Your father knows what he said, Jacky."

O-kay. Now the prettiest girl on the beach is jumping ugly in my face, too.

"Here's the new deal, Jacky," says my dad. "Whenever you have detention at school, you have a double detention at home. Do I make myself clear?"

"Not exactly. What's a d-d-double d-d-d—"

He doesn't wait for me to stutter it out.

"A double detention means for every hour of detention you serve at school, you come straight home and double that hour doing chores around the house."

"What k-k-kind of ch-ch-chores?"

"I've made a list."

He hands it to me.

Jeez-oh-man. They're the worst chores imagin-
able. Cleaning the oven. Washing windows. Ironing.
Dusting. Changing the kitty litter.

I look up. "We don't have a cat."

"Mrs. Rattner next door has three."

Riiiight.

So I walk home alone, wondering how everything
could go so wrong, so fast. Will Sandfleas, our dog,
turn against me if I start hanging out with cats?

And jeez—maybe it's just my imagination, but
Dad seemed awful chummy up in his chair with
Jenny Cornwall, the prettiest girl on the beach.

CHAPTER 12

Luckily, things don't stay totally bleak for long.

When I get home, it's time for the Fabulous Hart Sister Act.

First, we do our nightly chores. But since Dad is working late, we do them with a little more pizzazz.

We fix dinner. Hot dogs and baked beans with Tastykake Krimpets for dessert. Emma makes up the menu. (She's six, remember.) Hannah, the other middle child, does most of the cooking. I make most of the jokes.

I grab a wooden spoon and turn it into my microphone.

Even though I didn't ask (and neither did anybody else), Victoria gives me advice about my detentions, enlightens us on the history of mustard, and
tells us why we should all read *Joyful Noise: Poems
for Two Voices.*

"Even Sandfleas?" I crack.

The dog whimpers. She's not big on poetry.

We do the dishes assembly-line style and add in
some of Madonna's "Vogue" dance moves as Hannah
washes, Riley and I dry, Victoria and Sophia put

stuff away in the cupboards, and Emma bosses us all around.

Kitchen tidy, we launch into our nightly chatter while we do group homework. We spread out all over our tiny little living room—on the couch, on the floor, on our ratty old beanbag chair—and help each other with our schoolwork while simultaneously catching up on what happened in everybody's day. The conversation can be kind of confusing. In fact, if you aren't one of the Hart girls, you probably have no idea what any of us are talking about.

That first day of school, the Sister Act went something like this:

JACKY: So, Riley, do you have Mrs. Trefonas for sixth grade? Because I had her last year.

VICTORIA: I had her, years ago. And I think she spells her name wrong.

HANNAH: Years ago, I used to collect Cabbage Patch dolls. They were soooo cute.

JACKY: I believe *Mrs. Trefonas* means "Mrs. Three Telephones." Her ancestors had more phones than anyone in their village.

SOPHIA: If Mike Guadagno calls, don't answer the phone.

RILEY: How will we know if it's Mike Guadagno?

JACKY: The room will suddenly smell like Old Spice aftershave.

HANNAH: Nuh-uh. Eternity for Men. That's what Mike wears. It's from Calvin Klein.

SOPHIA: How did you know that?

EMMA: Who's Calvin Klein?

JACKY: A smelly man in tight blue jeans.

HANNAH: Anyone up for more dessert?

By the time we're finished gabbing, everybody's homework is not only done, it's also been thoroughly reviewed by someone who's already taken the class. Except for Sophia. Since she's a senior in high school and Sydney is off at college, Sophia is basically on her own.

We all stay up past our bedtimes, until we hear Dad crunch up our gravel-and-seashell driveway.

At ten p.m.

From his lifeguarding job?

Okay, that's a little weird. I mean, what kind of overtime is involved in guarding a dark, empty beach? "Hey, you. Yes, you, sand crab. No pinching allowed!"

By the way, this isn't the first time Dad's come home so late from "work."

And after seeing them sitting side by side up on that lifeguard chair, I have to wonder: Does Jenny Cornwall, the prettiest girl on the beach, have something to do with Dad's late nights?

CHAPTER 13

I ride Le Bike to school most days.

I call my bike Le Bike because I want to be one of zose French girls in ze movies, riding around with ze basket filled with ze fresh flowers and long, crusty loaves of bread. I'd wear a striped shirt and a jaunty beret and say, *"Bonjour,* Pierre," to everybody I met, even if zat is not their name. I would not, however, be a mime.

All in all, pedaling Le Bike is much more interesting than riding a bike, which is what Riley does, tagging along beside me.

Most kids who ride their bikes to school take all sorts of shortcuts. I always take the scenic route. Some days, I even take a detour to cruise the Seaside Heights boardwalk. Summer might be officially over, but that doesn't mean we can't still savor the September sunshine and salty air.

"We're going to be late," says Riley.

"You ever wonder why that statue of a guy holding an ax looks exactly like Alfred E. Neuman from *Mad* magazine?"

"Seriously, Jacky…"

"And what do they serve at that raw bar place? Drinks made out of uncooked hamburger meat?"

"It's seafood, Jacky. Raw clams, oysters…"

"Do you think the seagulls have a pooping point system? Like, old people are only worth one point because they're easy to hit, and babies are worth three because they're a smaller target?"

Riley finally laughs. "You're weird, Jacky."

"Thanks. I'll take that as a compliment."

I check out all the stuffed dolls hanging on pegboards behind the games of chance that aren't even open yet. It's a nice mix of Flintstones, Simpsons, and Jetsons.

"Do you think cartoons hang out with each other? If so, do you think the Jetsons make fun of the Flintstones' car? I mean, the Flintstones have to use their feet to drive—the Jetsons' cars fly."

We pass a closed souvenir shop that sells ships in bottles.

"Of course, the hardest part is getting all the tiny shipbuilders to crawl out of the bottle when they're finished building the boat."

Finally, we roll down a ramp and head off to school.

We're late, of course. By about thirty minutes.

"Why so tardy, Miss Hart?" asks Mrs. Turner, who's standing on the other side of the front door when we breeze into school. "Trouble at home?"

"Nope. Everything's hunky-dory. Just had a hankering for a funnel cake, so we stopped by the boardwalk."

"The boardwalk?"

"Yep. I get a better education there than in school, that's for sure."

Mrs. Turner gives me five more detentions. Because she can.

"You can start serving these along with your first five next Monday afternoon."

"Thanks," I say flippantly. "Something to look forward to."

"Am I getting detentions, too?" asks Riley sheepishly.

"No, Riley. You get a pass. It's not your fault that Jacqueline Hart is your sister."

CHAPTER 14

On Thursday, I come prepared to make somebody pay for what Mrs. Turner said to Riley.

That stuff about what a lousy sister I am.

I find an old cooler Dad keeps in the garage. It smells like fish guts, which will make my prank even better. I grab a can of spray paint and scrawl HUMAN HEAD on the side.

Next I find an old clipboard and make a fake sign-up sheet.

Before biology class starts, I sneak into the room and put the cooler on the front lab table.

On the chalkboard, I write: "Tomorrow, we will be dissecting a human head. The sign-up list is on my desk. Please indicate which part of the head you would most like to dissect."

Half the class and Mrs. Bollendorf, the biology teacher, freak out. She tacks on five more detentions to the ten I already have.

I guess I totally traumatized Mrs. Bollendorf with that "get to the head of the class" gag, because the next day, we have a substitute biology teacher named Mr. Kant.

Mr. Kant, the sub, thinks he's hysterical.

Nobody is laughing.

Except Kimberly Massimore. She'll laugh at anything.

"Now then," says Mr. Kant, smugly wiping his hands to get rid of chalk dust, "what were you kids studying with Mrs. Bollendorf?"

"The circulatory system," says Kimberly Massimore, batting her eyelashes. "Not the human head."

"Very good. The circulatory system. So you children already know the three kinds of blood vessels: arteries, veins, and caterpillars."

I groan. Loudly.

"Is there a problem, Miss…"

He looks down at his seating chart.

"Hart," I say to save him some time. "You know, like the organ that pumps blood through all those arteries, veins, and *capillaries*."

"Very good, Miss Hart," he says sarcastically. "Why, you must be Mrs. Bollendorf's favorite student of all time."

"Not after yesterday. If I knew she had such a weak stomach, I would've made her think we were dissecting rats or maggots…something less gross."

"Oh, you're that clever little girl I heard about in the faculty room—Jacky HeeHaw? The one who brought in the cooler with the 'human head' inside it?"

"Why? Are you missing your brain?"

"You might think you're a comedian, Jacky, but notice that no one else is laughing."

"Because they're all busy wondering why you bother trying to hide that huge bald spot!"

That gets a laugh. We duel with words for maybe ten minutes. Mr. Kant tries to top me, but, well, he *can't*. I'm getting way more laughs, so he pulls out his secret weapon.

You guessed it. The pink pad. He gives me another five detentions.

"It's totally unfair," I tell Mrs. Turner when I turn in my newest pink slip. "It was a battle of wits. And I won f-f-fair and square. Well, maybe it wasn't totally fair because Mr. Kant's a half-wit, but I got three times more laughs than he did."

"You also have more detentions than anybody in school," says Mrs. Turner. "Twenty. You racked up a whole month's worth in just five days."

"Four. I took Wednesday off."

"Impressive. You can start serving them, an hour at a time, on Monday. Unless..." She slides open her desk drawer and pulls out that stupid play script again. "They're holding auditions right now in the auditorium."

"No thanks. I'm not acting in any play."

"It's a musical."

"S-s-same thing. And Charlie Brown isn't a good man, he's an idiot. Lucy is always going to yank that football away whenever he tries to k-k-kick it."

Just like teachers will always think they're funnier than you are.

And they hate it when you prove them wrong.

AAAUGH!!

CHAPTER 15

Monday comes, and the good news is that I don't rack up any more detentions. The bad news? After classes, I head straight to room 102 to start serving my time.

You'd think I'd work harder to avoid detention hall, since some of the other hard-core offenders are mean, nasty, vicious kids who never really climbed aboard the "Jacky Ha-Ha = Class Clown" bandwagon. They just like tormenting me and my stutter.

"Wh-wh-why, look-k-k-k. It's Jac-ack-ack-ack..." says one, a guy I nicknamed Bubblebutt, even though he doesn't actually know that's what I call him.

His buddy, Ringworm (another secret nickname), picks up where Bubblebutt left off: "Ack-key-key-key."

Then they do a little duet on the "Ha-Ha-Ha-Hart."

fig 1: Bubblebutt   fig 2: Ringworm

"Good afternoon, idiots," I say. "Wh-wh-what are you guys in here for? Mispronouncing your own names?"

"We're here because we like to make dumb, stuttering girls c-c-c-cry," Bubblebutt says, cracking his knuckles. His little shadow, Ringworm, cracks his, too.

"How? By burning off their eyebrows with your bad breath?"

It's been a while since I did some real trash-talking, and I know I can wipe the floor with Bubblebutt and his lapdog. I got plenty of practice this summer when

I played catcher on an all-boys Little League baseball team. I spent every game crouching behind home plate and swapping insults with all the boys batting for the other team. I loved it.

Before we can really get started, though, the door swings open and a woman strides into the room.

It's the new English teacher, Ms. O'Mara. The one who's directing the Charlie Brown musical. The one who used to be a child star on Broadway, which, frankly, is pretty hard for me to imagine because Ms. O'Mara looks like she's at least thirty-something years old.

Welcome to Detention Hall. My name is Ms. O'Mara. Kindly take your seats, but don't take them too far because we're going to need them.

Ms. O'Mara goes to the desk at the front of the room and picks up the detention list.

"Jacky Hart?"

Guess my name is at the top.

"Here."

"Ah, there you are. We missed you at auditions last week. Mrs. Turner told me to keep an eye out for you."

"Sorry. I don't want to get up on stage and sing about what a good man Charlie Brown is. The kid is bald."

"I know," says Ms. O'Mara. "But he tries to do a comb-over with that one spit curl he has up front."

I try to shock her. "And Snoopy looks dead on top of the doghouse."

"Really? I think he looks like Michelangelo, painting the ceiling of the Sistine Chapel."

"Which," I say, "was a pretty dumb way to paint a ceiling."

"I know," says Ms. O'Mara. "You'd get paint in your eyes."

"You'd roll around on your scaffold, screaming 'I can't see what I'm painting!' Then you'd tumble over the edge, fall to the floor, and die. Unless the floor was actually a trampoline."

"True. That's why I only paint ceilings in bouncy houses."

"They had an inflatable bouncy castle at the church carnival once until I ruined it. Guess I should've taken off my baseball cleats before I jumped in."

And then neither one of us says anything—even though all the kids in the room are cracking up, even the hard-core repeat offenders.

Who is this new teacher? I wonder. What strange and magical powers does she possess that she can take my funny and make it funnier but then bounce it back to me?

Have I finally met my match?

"By the way, Jacky," says Ms. O'Mara, "I caught your act on the boardwalk."

"Huh?"

"Last day of summer? Technicolor rainbow?" She uses her hands to mime puke exploding out of her mouth. "You have a lot of stage presence."

"No, I had a lot of junk food."

"But you held that crowd, Jacky. Had them right in the palm of your hand. That's not easy to do. Meredith tells me you do it all the time."

"You know Meredith Crawford?"

"Yep. She's up for Lucy in *Charlie Brown*. The girl can sing like an angel."

"I sing more like an elephant."

"Doesn't matter. You'd be a good Snoopy. Funniest part in the show."

"But I told you—I c-c-can't sing."

"It's true," says Bubblebutt. "She k-k-keeps adding extra n-n-notes."

Ms. O'Mara eases around and stares the creep down. "Why are you here, young man? Shouldn't you be home watching *Thomas the Tank Engine* with the rest of the kids in your kindergarten class?"

"I-I-I..." Bubblebutt is the one sputtering now.

"*Gesundheit*," says Ms. O'Mara. She turns to face me again. "Snoopy doesn't really have to sing. You can kind of talk-sing through it—if you have enough stage presence, which you do, Jacky. Besides, if you're at play practice, you can't be in detention." She looks at the detention list. "Yowzer. Twenty detentions? Already?"

I shrug. "I'm an overachiever."

"Okay. Here's the deal." She folds up the detention sheet and stuffs it into the pocket of her skirt. "One play practice equals one detention. We'll have twenty rehearsals and four performances."

"That's twenty-four. Do I get four Get Out of Jail Free cards?"

"I'll talk to Mrs. Turner. See what we can work out. Plus, you can't earn any *new* detentions. So what do you say, Jacky? Are you in or out? Because if you're in, I'm letting you out."

I look around. Bubblebutt and Ringworm stare back at me with equal parts stupidity and menace on their pasty faces.

So what do I have to lose except twenty torturous detentions…and my last shred of dignity when an entire audience laughs *at* me, not with me?

Still, there's something about Ms. O'Mara.

And if Meredith might be in the show...

"I'm in," I finally say.

"Good!" says Ms. O'Mara.

That's when Coach Harris, the gym teacher, lumbers into the room. The man has so many muscles he doesn't have a neck, just a head stump.

"Sorry I'm late," he says. "Guess I should give myself a detention. Oh, hi, Ms. O'Mara. What're you doing here?"

"Jacky and I got lost," she says, taking me by my elbow. "I'm still so new to this building. We were looking for the auditorium?"

"It's down the hall and to the right."

"Thank you."

Coach Harris is fumbling around on the desk. "Did you see the detention sheet, Ms. O'Mara?"

"Nope. But I think everybody in this room knows exactly why they're here. Come on, Jacky."

We hurry out the door.

"You're not in charge of detention?" I whisper when we hit the hall.

"What?" deadpans Ms. O'Mara. "Do you think you're the only one at this school who likes to pull pranks?"

CHAPTER 16

Of course I'm smiling like crazy as I march down the hall with Ms. O'Mara.

I've never had a teacher bust me out of detention before. We're moving pretty briskly because Ms. O'Mara does everything with oomph. She probably even *sleeps* in a hurry.

"So," I say as we bustle down the hall toward the auditorium, which is all the way over on the other side of the building, "can I ask you a favor?"

"You can ask, Jacky, but I'm not a genie, so there's no guarantee I'll be able to grant your wish."

"By the way," I say, before I get around to asking my real question, "do you ever wonder why everybody who rubs a genie lamp doesn't just use one of their first three wishes to ask for like three million more?"

"All the time," says Ms. O'Mara. "But you know what I'd ask for, probably on wish number two?"

"What?"

"The ability to grant my *own* wishes—with no limitations."

"Why wouldn't you ask for that first?"

"I wouldn't want the genie to think I'm greedy. So what's your magic wish, Jacky?"

"That you write a note to my dad and let him know about our detention–play practice swap agreement."

"Why?"

"He has me on this double detention deal. Every hour of detention I serve, I have to serve another hour at home. Cleaning toilets."

"Really?" says Ms. O'Mara, sounding shocked. "How many toilets do you guys have?"

"Just the one."

"And it takes you an hour to clean it?"

"No, but there are other toilet-level chores, like oven scrubbing, freezer defrosting, kitty litter scooping, bathtub drain dehairing—"

"I get it," interrupted Ms. O'Mara. "Fine. If you get into the show, I'll write the note."

"If I...? I thought I was already in the cast."

"I hope so. I mean, *I* definitely want you to play Snoopy. You're absolutely my first choice. But…"

"B-b-but what?"

"Well, first you have to convince my musical director, Mr. Brimer. He thinks Dan Napolitano should be the one to play Snoopy, but I like Dan better for Schroeder. And then there's Mrs. Yen…."

"The g-g-gym teacher?"

Ms. O'Mara nods. "She's my choreographer."

"There's c-c-choreography? I have to d-d-dance?"

Ms. O'Mara holds up her finger and thumb to show me a half inch of empty air. "Little bit."

"B-b-but I can't dance…."

"That's okay, Jacky. Just as long as you move well."

"Move well? What does that mean?"

"Well." Ms. O'Mara puts her hand on the auditorium door. "It means you kind of, sort of have to dance."

CHAPTER 17

Ms. O'Mara leads the way into the semidark auditorium.

I'm scared to death, but I'm also kind of excited.

To tell you the truth, I still feel the same way every time I step onto a stage or in front of the cameras. Terrified and electrified, all at the same time. Those butterflies beating their wings against the walls of my stomach never go away.

They also never shut up.

They scream all the way up to the inside of my head (usually in a very loud, nasally voice because butterflies have those long pollen-snorting snouts), saying, "Go on, Jacky! Get out there. Show 'em they're wrong. Show 'em you can do this! Show 'em you're better than they think you are."

My stomach butterflies are, basically, my semi-psychotic cheerleaders.

Mrs. Yen, the plucky phys ed teacher and gymnastics coach who always reminds me of Peter Pan, is sitting in the front row.

Mrs. Yen is wearing workout clothes. I'm in shorts and a red T-shirt from the Gap.

Up onstage, I see Mr. Brimer, sitting on a bench in front of a battered upright piano.

Mr. Brimer, who teaches chorus and band, is lean

and lanky. He wears those glasses that turn dark in the sun and clear when you're indoors, but they never actually undarken all the way, so he always looks mysterious behind tinted shades. He has his legs crossed so he can prop his elbow on a knee and rest his chin on his hand and look bored and irked at the same time. I think we've kept him waiting a little too long.

"Sorry we're late," says Ms. O'Mara, coming down the center aisle behind me. "I had to spring Jacky out of jail."

Mr. Brimer flutters open some sheet music propped up on the ledge above his keyboard. "'Suppertime' from the top?"

I have no idea what he's talking about.

"Sounds good," says Mrs. Yen, springing up out of her seat, stretching sideways, and cracking her neck.

"Here are your sides, Jacky," says Ms. O'Mara, grabbing a stack of paper off a seat.

One thing I learned pretty quickly about "thee-ah-tah" people: they use a lot of backstage lingo. For instance, *strike the set* means "take down the scenery," not "grab a protest sign and start a labor dispute."

Sides, I discover, are not the mashed potatoes, creamed corn, or French fries that come with your main course. In the theater, *sides* means a short selection from the script on cue cards.

"I'll read Charlie Brown's lines," says Ms. O'Mara.

I look at the script. "So, I, um, I read Sn-n-n-noopy?"

Mr. Brimer gives me a very aggravated chord of sour notes.

"Hello?" he says (dramatically, of course, since these are the drama club auditions). "There are only two parts in this scene. Snoopy and Charlie Brown."

"And WHISTLES," I say, because I see the word typed in all caps halfway down the page.

I earn another jarring chord—mostly black keys.

"That, my dear girl, is a stage direction! You whistle that part. Honestly..."

I just nod. And kind of stare at Mr. Brimer.

And the little butterflies down in my stomach start screaming into my head again. "Show him, Jacky! Show him who you are!"

So I do.

CHAPTER 18

I *kill it.*

Sorry. That's more backstage lingo.

Killing it has nothing to do with murder or mayhem. It means you nailed your lines and cracked up the audience.

First, I do a quivery-voiced, melodramatic rendition of Snoopy complaining about how he'll probably die of starvation because Charlie Brown forgot to feed him. I only stutter maybe once on the first letter of the first word. It's an *M*.

*M*s are tough.

But the more I "get into character," the less I worry about stammering or stumbling across the consonants.

So I really throw myself into the role. I thrash around in agony.

Mr. Brimer's piano is backing me up with a very melancholy "dum-dee-dum-dum"-style funeral dirge. The music makes me emote even more. They call being hammy onstage "chewing the scenery." Since I'm playing a dog, I figure chewing on stuff is okay.

Ms. O'Mara reads out Charlie Brown's lines about bringing me my supper bowl and water dish. I decide to treat the arrival of my food as the greatest achievement in the history of the world. I sing my first couple of lyrics like it's a grand opera, complete with dramatic yodeling.

Behold The Brimming Bowl

Ms. O'Mara was right. I can talk-sing and mug my way through Snoopy's number. When I'm done mocking opera, I move into a pretty good mime act, opening invisible doors and bumping into walls that aren't there.

"Keep it nice and easy, Jacky," Mrs. Yen coaches. "Just feel the beat in your feet."

I slip and slide across the stage and wave my one free arm around a little because the other arm is busy holding my sides (meaning, of course, the sheet of paper with my lines and lyrics, not my rib cage).

I pantomime that I snatch up my dog food bowl and start twirling it around like I'm dancing with it. I pretend to be slinging loose kibble all over the place because I know Charlie Brown is going to come in and tell me to "CUT THAT OUT!" so I really want to give him something to scream about.

It's wild. Being Snoopy, I get to be the me I wish I could sometimes be—especially when Dad starts yelling at me, telling me to "STOP THAT, JACKY!" and all I want to do is keep dizzily spinning along, spiraling out of control.

Ms. O'Mara reads Charlie Brown's line, which, basically, asks why Snoopy can't be calm like most other dogs.

To which I, as Snoopy, reply, "So what's wrong with making mealtime a joyous occasion?"

When I say that, I really, really, *really* want to be in the show.

I do my last stanza of "*Supper, supper, supper, suppertime!*" without caring that I'm acting nuttier than a porta-potty at a peanut festival.

Mrs. Yen and Ms. O'Mara applaud. It's only two people so the applause sounds a little pitter-patterish, but I love it.

Mr. Brimer closes up his sheet music and squeaks down the lid to cover the piano keys.

"Fine," he says. "Dan Napolitano is Schroeder. Jacky is our Snoopy. But please, Miss Hart—in the future, be on time."

CHAPTER 19

Because of my mini-detention and last-minute audition, I'm a little late coming home from school.

But I'm not the only one who's late.

It's way after six and Dad isn't home.

"Where is he?" wonders Sophia in her role as the oldest-sister-still-living-at-home-and-therefore-in-charge-of-everything-including-worrying. "Is the beach still even open after Labor Day?"

"No," says Victoria, because she knows all the municipal rules and regulations better than the mayor of Seaside Heights. "The last day of the season is, officially, Labor Day, and even then, lifeguards are only on duty from ten in the morning until five at night, weather permitting. However, since Dad is the head lifeguard, he has other responsibilities, such as..."

As usual, Victoria babbles on. And, as usual, nobody listens to her.

"I wonder if there was a big cruise ship wreck somewhere," says Sophia, even more dramatically than Mr. Brimer would. "What if Dad had to go help rescue people?"

"I hope he remembered to take his paddleboard," I crack.

We go back and forth about Dad for maybe thirty minutes. Everybody has a theory. Pretty soon, we're popping some microwave popcorn to tide us over until suppertime (yes, I almost break into Snoopy's

big number) because none of us knows when supper-time might actually be. We always try to eat dinner as a family, but that's extremely difficult when the "head of the family" is working late doing paperwork about shark bites. Or something.

While we're passing around the popcorn bowl, Sophia changes the subject to her favorite topic: *boys*.

"So, Chad and I are going to the movies next weekend. He wants to see *Die Hard 2* but I want to see *Ghost*."

I raise my hand. "Um, hello? Who's Chad?"

"This guy I'm dating. He goes to Rutgers Prep."

"What happened to Mike Guadagno?" With Sophia, it's hard to keep up with the boy parade.

Sophia shrugs. "Mike was nice. But Chad is *dreamy*."

"I still like Mike," says Hannah. "I think he's dreamy, too."

"I'm hungry," Emma, the Little Boss, blurts out.

"We should wait for Dad," suggests Hannah.

"We've *been* waiting for Dad," says Riley.

"I think we're past the two-hour rule," I say, checking out the kitchen clock. It's nearly seven.

"Should we call the police?" says Hannah.

"No," says Emma. "We should call the pizza guys."

Emma bulldozes her way across the kitchen to the wall phone. (Yes, back then, we actually bolted telephones to walls, and the handsets were attached to their base by long, curled cords. Weird, huh?) She speed-dials Three Brothers from Italy Pizza, our family fave, I guess because we're Seven Sisters from Seaside Heights. Emma's order is the same as it always is: two plain cheese pizzas.

Emma hangs up the phone and opens up the

cookie jar, where Dad and Mom keep our "emergency cash."

"Dinner will be here in thirty minutes," she announces. "Everybody finish your homework and wash your hands."

The pizza shows up around seven thirty.

Dad?

He doesn't show up until after eleven.

CHAPTER 20

The next morning at school, Meredith Crawford comes running up to me the second I set foot in the building.

"I didn't know you were auditioning for *Charlie Brown!*"

"Me neither."

"We both got in!"

"Really?"

"I'm Lucy, you're Snoopy. Ms. O'Mara just posted the cast list on her door."

Meredith grabs me by the arm and hustles me down the hall to where a crowd of kids has formed a tight semicircle. One or two squeal and bounce up and down. Others slump their shoulders, clearly wishing they had invisibility cloaks, and quietly slink away.

"Come on," says Meredith, elbowing her way through the mob.

"Hey, watch it," snaps a blond girl named Beth Bennett, who's never been very nice to me.

"Sorry," says Meredith.

"You should be," mutters Beth as she spins around and pushes her way out of the mob. She's kind of huffy and puffy about it, too. The last thing I hear her say is "I wanted Lucy, not Patty."

BETH LEAVES IN A **HUFF**

"See?" says Meredith. She points at a sheet of paper Scotch-taped under the little rectangular window on Ms. O'Mara's classroom door.

And there it is. A simple typed list that, more or less, changes my whole life.

```
CHARLIE BROWN—Bill Phillips
SCHROEDER—Dan Napolitano
LUCY VAN PELT—Meredith Crawford
LINUS VAN PELT—Jeff Cohen
PATTY—Beth Bennett
SNOOPY—Jacky Hart
LITTLE RED-HAIRED GIRL—Somebody
WOODSTOCK—Somebody Else
CHORUS—A Whole Bunch of Other People
```

To be honest, there are a couple of characters and a whole boatload of chorus people listed after me, but I don't even know if they have names. All I really see are Meredith's name and mine.

```
LUCY VAN PELT—Meredith Crawford
SNOOPY—Jacky Hart
```

Time shifts into super slo-mo and I stare at our names for hours.

Okay, it's really about fifteen seconds.

"Way to go, Bill," I hear some kids say as they clap a cute guy on his back.

"Will you still help me with my math homework now that you're a star?" some other guy says to him.

Bill laughs and says, "I'll try to squeeze you in."

"Hi, Bill," says Meredith, because she's sort of bold that way. Me? I may act crazy in public, but I'm actually very shy.

"Hey," says Bill.

"I'm Meredith. Meredith Crawford. Congratulations on Charlie Brown."

"Thanks. Same to you. I heard you sing at the auditions. Man, your Lucy is going to be incredible."

"Thanks! Oh, this is my friend Jacky. She's Snoopy."

Bill smiles but looks confused. "I don't remember seeing you at auditions...."

"She had a family thing," says Meredith. "So they auditioned her yesterday, right?"

"Yeah," I say. "Y-y-yesterday."

"Cool," says Bill. A bell rings. "Guess we better head to class. See you two at rehearsal tomorrow. Break a leg."

"Huh?" I snap, wondering why a nice boy I just met would wish me bodily harm.

Meredith takes my elbow again and guides me up the hall.

"It's a theater thing," she explains. *"Break a leg* means good luck."

"Seriously? In what world is a broken leg a sign of good luck?"

"In the theater, *break a leg* means 'I hope you're so good you'll be bending your knee a lot when you take all those bows after the audience gives you a standing ovation.'"

"Why don't they just say 'good luck'?" I ask.

"Because it's bad luck."

Wow. Theater people are even weirder than *me*.

Hankie optional

Note bending or Breaking a leg.

CHAPTER 21

At lunchtime, Meredith and I are sitting at our usual table. An eighth grader named Colleen comes to join us. I've never actually met her before, but she has her wallet on a thick silver chain clipped to her belt, so she's hard not to notice.

"You two are in the show, right?" Colleen asks. She keeps her hair cut so short, she'd fit right in with Mom and the marines.

"Yes," I say. "I'm playing Snoopy. Meredith's Lucy."

"I'm Colleen. I'm a techie. Lights and sets."

"Cool," says Meredith, scooting over so Colleen can sit next to her.

Colleen doesn't say much else. She just dives into her watery pudding cup.

All of a sudden, at the table behind us, I hear a gaggle of giggles.

It's Beth Bennett, the girl who wanted to play Lucy, surrounded by a bevy of Beth wannabes.

"I feel sorriest for Jeff Cohen," Beth tells her clique. "He's playing Linus. Lucy's supposed to be his sister. How's that going to look? I mean, in the comic strip, Lucy only has black *hair*."

Her whole table titter-giggles.

"I guess this is why the show is called *You're a Good Man, Charlie...Brown!*"

Meredith drops her eyes and focuses on her sandwich.

The fact that Meredith is African-American isn't something I ever really think about, but now I suddenly realize this is just a single scrap of the trash she probably listens to regularly. I'm tempted to spin around and verbally rip Little Miss Blondie to shreds. Then I remember that fighting in the cafeteria comes with a mandatory minimum sentence of five detentions, and if I score just one more, I'm out of the show.

"You want me to go have a word with that idiot?" Colleen asks Meredith.

"That's okay. I'm used to it."

"I'm not," I say.

I stand up. Turn around. Then I smile my sweetest smile. "We're all so glad you're in the show, Beth. Break a leg. *Both* of them."

Colleen and Meredith snort-laugh chocolate milk out their noses.

I see Ms. O'Mara passing behind our table. She locks eyes with me for a second, and I'm sure she's going to stop and whip out her pink pad of doom, but she sails on by without stopping. Wait, did she just wink at me?

Maybe you *can* fight for what's right without ending up in detention hall. You just need to find the right words.

CHAPTER 22

Ms. O'Mara gives me a copy of the *Charlie Brown* script right after the final bell.

"Read it tonight," she says. "Mark your lines. Our first rehearsal tomorrow will be a read-through with all the leads."

"Okay," I say, fully intending to read the play as soon as I get home, but there's a letter waiting for me.

It's from Mom.

My mother is very creative with her letter writing. Somehow, in the midst of doing whatever it takes to be battle-ready over there in Saudi Arabia, she finds the time to write each and every one of us,

including Dad, a separate letter. Then she puts all
eight of them into a bigger envelope. She does this
every week, without fail.

My personalized
envelope has
something
else tucked
inside. A tiny
plastic bag filled with
Saudi Arabian sand. Since we
live so close to a beach, this is a bizarro
collection I started when I was three. Sand from
around the globe.

So far I've got New Jersey. Lots of New Jersey. Most of the beaches up and down the shore. A cousin sent me some sand from Marina del Rey, California. And now Mom has added the Middle East. Okay, it's a small collection. Someday, I think, I'll make a couple of egg timers out of it.

My mother, aka Big Sydney, is a staff sergeant in the Marine Corps with an Air Control Group. They're sort of like air traffic controllers for fighter planes and bombers. In her letter this week, she tells me about her bus rides to the control tower, about thirty minutes away from her base and barracks.

"The buses are always packed," she writes. "Worse than New York City at rush hour. And riding on the Saudi highway is no picnic. Especially when it's one hundred and seven degrees in the shade... except there's absolutely no shade. Just sand. For the full effect, put the sample I sent you in the microwave. No, don't. Forget I wrote that."

"I miss you guys like crazy, and I don't want you worrying about me. We're miles away from where any real fighting might take place. The bad news is, we don't know when Uncle Sam will send us home.

The good news? I've already picked out my Halloween costume for next year."

Clipped to the letter is a photo.

Of Mom in her gas mask.

It's funny. And scary.

Because everybody knows Saddam Hussein, as evil as he is, has used poison gas before. *On his own people.*

The bug woman from outer space!

When I write to Mom, which I do at least once a week (and sometimes twice or three times), I try to be light and positively "Jacky Ha-Ha," just like her.

I write about Riley and Emma and the silly stuff they've done that's crazy cute. I write about Sophia's rotating boyfriends and soap opera love life. And Hannah's continuing crush on Mike Guadagno. I let Mom know what I learned from Victoria this week and why I'll never play Trivial Pursuit against her.

I skip the part about my twenty detentions (I figure that's on a need-to-know basis and she definitely doesn't need to know, at least from me). Instead, I tell her that I tried out for (and got into) the school play and how much fun I'm going to have, because I know she'd love that.

But secretly? Just between us?

When I'm alone, behind a closed bedroom door, working on my letters to Mom, I start to cry when I think about how much I miss her. And when I think about her being halfway around the world in a place so sweltering hot and dangerous, I cry even harder.

My mother might try to keep things light and fluffy in her letters, but I know the truth: She's currently in what sounds like the most dangerous place on earth.

So no way am I mentioning Dad's late nights or how he doesn't come home for dinner like he's supposed to.

That would just make Saudi Arabia even more miserable for Mom.

I finish my letter and move on to something even more depressing.

Homework.

CHAPTER 23

English is my first class in the morning.

Ms. O'Mara, as you might recall, teaches Honors English. I am not in Honors English, even though English happens to be my best subject.

Okay. It *used* to be my best subject.

All of a sudden, I'm flunking it. Pulling a big fat F.

I went into Mrs. Bucci's classroom that day with an A-minus or maybe a B-plus average.

Okay, I had a B-minus. But it was a *solid* B-minus.

Then Mrs. Bucci read my essay on *The Short Stories of Nathaniel Hawthorne*.

I don't think she likes the fact that I spent my first two paragraphs writing about how Hawthorne added a *W* to his last name so he wouldn't be connected to his Hathorne ancestors, who were involved in the Salem witch trials.

"In the same manner," I wrote, "I might change my last name to Hawrt, if, say, my sister Sophia seriously starts dating this preppy guy named Chad. Chad is not a person. It's a country in Africa."

"Miss Hart?" Mrs. Bucci says over the edge of her reading glasses after she finishes glancing at my essay. "Did you read any of the short stories or just the author's name?"

"The s-s-stories."

Right away, I start stuttering.

Mrs. Bucci knows I read the material. But she really doesn't like my attitude, so she keeps coming at me.

"What was in Dr. Heidegger's study?"

I crack a joke. "St-st-st-uff for him to study."

She writes something at the top of my paper. "C-plus. Want to go down another grade? Maybe go for two?"

"H-h-he also had a sk-sk-skeleton in his closet," I say, which, by the way, is correct. But I can't stand the fact that Mrs. Bucci just made me so nervous I'm stuttering in front of my seventh-grade English class, so I add, "How m-m-many skeletons are in *your* closet, Mrs. Bucci?"

The class cracks up. Mrs. Bucci does not.

"Let's make that a D-plus," she says.

"F-f-fine. By the way, in the story, Dr. H-H-Heidegger f-f-found the fountain of youth. It was in Florida." I take a beat. Study Mrs. Bucci's wrinkled face. "You've never been to Florida, have you, Mrs. Bucci?"

More "ha-has" for me, another step down for my grade.

"F-plus. No, wait. Let's make it an even F."

I still don't stop. *"F* f-for *funny?"*

"No, Jacky. For *failure*. Complete and hopeless."

The bell rings. Everyone races for the door.

"Jacky, come here."

"Y-y-yes, Mrs. Bucci?" I ask, very politely. Remember how Ms. O'Mara said I'm not allowed to get any more detentions, or I'm out of the school play? Well, neither did I, until that moment. Better late than never.

"Be careful of your urge to entertain, Jacky,"

Mrs. Bucci warns as if she is a spooky oracle straight out of Greek mythology. "Beware of wanting to be liked too much."

I just nod, because she's creeping me out.

"You have the gift of making others laugh, but don't forget about your own happiness. Is everything all right, Jacky?" she asks suddenly.

"Uh, yes?" Usually it's obvious what answer you're supposed to give, but I'm a little lost because this conversation just took a right turn into Weirdsville.

Mrs. Bucci sighs. "No more antics from now on. You may go."

I walk out feeling good that I didn't get another detention.

And what's so wrong about wanting to be liked? It's a lot better than *not* being liked, right?

Teachers.

CHAPTER 24

make it through another day with no detentions.

Our first rehearsal starts in the auditorium fifteen minutes after school is out. The show's six leads, all the actors with lines, are supposed to sit in a circle at center stage. Mr. Brimer, his chin propped in his hand again, is off to our left at his upright piano.

I'm sitting between Meredith and Bill (our Charlie Brown). Beth Bennett, who's playing Patty, is seated directly opposite me on the other side of the circle. She's between Dan Napolitano (Schroeder) and Jeff Cohen (Linus). Dan is so skinny, he'd probably blow away in a strong gust of wind. Jeff is a bundle of nervous energy, curly hair, and quirky eye tics.

"I brought a blanket," he says, his left eye seeming to stutter the way my tongue does. "Linus always has his security blanket, so I brought one even though this is just a read-through and not a run-through. The blanket might help me get into character."

We all just nod.

Except Beth Bennett. She exhales audibly. Looks at her watch. If she were chewing gum, she'd probably snap-pop it, too.

At precisely 3:15 p.m., Ms. O'Mara strides out of the wings (those are the sides of the stage that are hidden by the curtains, not a greasy bucket of spicy chicken bits).

"Good afternoon, everybody," she says. "And congratulations. The competition for these six roles was pretty intense. So give yourselves a round of applause."

We do. It's fun.

"Before we start our first read-through," she continues, "I want to warm up your ears. Because listening to your fellow cast members—really, sincerely *listening*—is a very important part of acting. Meredith?"

"Yes, Ms. O'Mara?"

"I don't mean to put you on the spot, but could you sing your Schroeder song for us?"

"Right now?"

"If you don't mind. I want the cast to hear it. To really *listen* to it."

"Come on, Meredith," says Mr. Brimer as he starts plunking out the opening notes of Beethoven's *Moonlight* Sonata on his keyboard. "Don't be modest. Show these guys what you've got."

Meredith smiles and pops out of her chair.

"This ought to be good," I hear Beth mutter to Jeff Cohen, who shushes her. She gives him an eye roll.

Meredith scampers over to the piano and leans on it with both arms, the way Lucy always leans on Schroeder's baby grand in the comic strips.

The *Moonlight* Sonata piano vamp keeps looping while Meredith glides into her lyrics.

"D'ya know something, Schroeder? I think the way you play the piano is nice."

Wow. It is so stunningly simple and beautiful. I mean, I've only known Meredith for a couple of months, and we didn't do much singing over the summer except when we were goofing on Vanilla Ice's horrible hit, "Ice Ice Baby," but I never realized she was so talented. She sings like an angel, just like Ms. O'Mara said. The one God would send down to earth for the first Christmas so she could sing "The First Noel" to certain shepherds in fields where they lay.

We're all mesmerized by her unbelievable voice.

And then, BOOM! Meredith nails the joke at the end of the song, too.

First she bats her eyes flirtatiously at Mr. Brimer and sings her final line:

"Wouldn't you like that if someday we two should get married?"

Mr. Brimer plays along, pretends to be horrified at the thought of marrying Lucy, and slams her a sour chord (the same one he slammed me for real at the audition). And Meredith, channeling Queen Lucy of the comic strips, sighs and says, "My aunt

Marion was right. Never try to discuss marriage with a musician."

The whole cast cracks up and starts clapping like crazy.

"That was awesome!" says Bill Phillips.

"Incredible," adds Jeff Cohen.

I'm pumping my arm up and down and *woo-hoo-ing* a lot.

Then Beth Bennett runs up. After all those mean, ugly, and downright despicable things she said about Meredith yesterday, I get ready to jump in and defend my best friend again.

I guess she's been converted. Or redeemed. Maybe both.

"So, Meredith," Beth says after finally breaking out of her congratulatory bear hug, "do you, like, give singing lessons? Could you be my vocal coach?"

Meredith grins. "We'll talk."

When we finally sit back down, the entire cast is pumped. We're excited to jump into our read-through. We're also feeling like one big, happy family.

I catch Ms. O'Mara's eye and she winks, just like she did in the cafeteria.

You see why Ms. O'Mara is so good at what she does?

She knows how to teach a lesson without "*teaching a lesson.*"

CHAPTER 25

B y the end of the week, I've traded in three after-school rehearsals for three detentions.

And I don't have to do extra chores every day after school because Ms. O'Mara sent me home with a note, explaining our arrangement to my dad: "So long as Jacqueline Hart shows up for play practice on time, does her best, and, at the same time, does not earn any NEW detentions, we will deduct one detention for every rehearsal. Perhaps you might consider also releasing Jacky from her 'double detentions' at home, too. She needs that time to do her homework and then memorize her lines."

Dad agrees.

So now, every night, after we finish our home-work, all the sisters help me "run my lines."

Sandfleas, our dog, is helping out, too.

On our nightly walks, she gives me all sorts of pointers on playing Snoopy. How to scratch behind my ear. How to circle three times before peeing. How to sniff other dogs' butts. It's like homework, only grosser.

I've even taken to singing "Suppertime" whenever I bring out Sandfleas's food dish or refill her water bowl. What's very interesting is that, after only three rehearsals, when I'm playing Snoopy or singing one of Snoopy's songs, I don't stutter.

It's the Mel Tillis effect.

Mel Tillis is a big country-western singer who had his heyday in the 1970s with a bunch of songs that shot up to the top of the charts. He even won the Country Music Association's Entertainer of the Year award.

He also had a stutter. In fact, he called his 1984 autobiography *Stutterin' Boy*. But his stutter never interfered with his singing. He never stumbled over a single note. Somehow, he was able to just shut it off.

And when I'm playing Snoopy, I can, too.

So I'm feeling pretty great on Monday morning when it's time to head back to school. I've memorized all my lines in the opening number.

Okay, so I just have to say "Woof." Three times.

Between classes, Mrs. Turner catches me in the halls.

Assistant Principals SELDOM Smile.

SOMETHING'S UP

"Ms. O'Mara tells me you're doing great, Jacky."

"You were right, it's fun. I'm glad I tried out for the show."

Assistant principals all over the world beam whenever a student tells them they were right about something (especially if the student used to think they were heinously wrong).

"And no new detentions," says Mrs. Turner, checking a file folder where, I guess, she keeps her Jacky Ha-Ha scorecard. "Good work, Jacky."

"Well, I made a solemn vow. On top of a Ferris wheel, too."

"Excuse me?"

"Nothing."

"Jacky?"

Uh-oh.

Why do I have the feeling that Mrs. Turner has dreamt up another crazy idea for me, to go along with the whole "be in the school play" thing?

"I want you to see Mrs. Jordan today."

"The social studies teacher?"

"She's also the debate team coach. I want you to enter the school oratory contest."

For once in my life, I'm speechless. *Oratory contest?*

Ignoring the dumbstruck look on my face, Mrs. Turner continues. "The contest takes place a few days before *Charlie Brown* opens, so you should be able to do both. I'll talk to Ms. O'Mara to work out any schedule conflicts."

"B-b-but…"

"I have to run. Keep up the good work, Jacky. We're all very proud of you."

I watch Mrs. Turner walk away while my jaw bangs against the floor.

Is she nuts?

I don't like the sound of this. At all. I have a feeling that an oratory contest means the contestants have to make sp-sp-speeches in front of an audience. My stutter might miraculously go away when I sing, but talking about boring stuff to a roomful of grown-ups doesn't have the same magic powers.

So I decide to blow off Mrs. Jordan. It should be no big deal. I'm sure she has more than enough kids from her debate team for the oratory contest.

Because no way am I getting up in front of an auditorium full of p-p-people to make a sp-sp-speech.

Not without Snoopy to hide behind.

CHAPTER 26

At play practice that afternoon, Ms. O'Mara tells us we have to be "off book" in two weeks. That means we have to memorize all our songs and lines in fourteen days! I have a long monologue that takes up a whole page in the script—and a monologue means I'm the only one talking. It's all about Snoopy pretending to be a World War One flying ace soaring high over France searching for his enemy, the Red Baron.

Bill Phillips has it worse. He has a ton of monologues.

"Too bad the speeches can't rhyme like the songs do," Bill says when he, Meredith, Jeff Cohen, and I are walking home after rehearsal.

"Indeed!" I say, getting goofy with a fake British accent. "It would be sublime if they, too, did rhyme."

Jeff builds on my bit. "Memorizing speeches? I'd rather have my blood sucked by leeches."

I grin because Jeff just gave me a great idea for a new stunt.

There just happens to be a McDonald's on our walk home from school. "Let's go in there and rhyme 'em!" I say. "First person who can't think of a rhyme has to pay for everybody else's milk shake!"

"I'll gladly partake!" says Jeff Cohen.

"I'll do it for Shakespeare's sake," adds Bill Phillips.

"I think this is a big mistake," says Meredith, who, don't forget, has been down this road with me before. "But I'll do anything for the sake of a creamy, frosty shake!"

Laughing, we run into Mickey Dee's and find the shortest line.

"May I take your order, please?" asks the chipper counter girl.

"Yes," says Jeff, going first. "The McDLT. What exactly is in it for me?"

"It has lettuce and tomatoes," says Bill, before the counter kid can. "Order it with some French-fried potatoes."

"I think I want the Happy Meal McDino," I say. "That triceratops toy looks like a rhino."

"I just want to attack a Big Mac," says Meredith. "For a snack."

We keep this up for about five minutes. It's hysterical. Well, *we* think it is. The counter girl? Not so much.

"Are you guys ever going to order anything?" she asks.

"I'll just have a small Coke," I say. "Nothing else, because I'm broke."

"Here, take it and go!" she snaps.

"You sure you don't want that Happy Meal before we leave?" says Bill as we head for the door.

Jeff, Meredith, and I stop and stare at him.

"What?" Bill says. "I thought you wanted the toy."

"And we have a loser!" I shout.

"I meant…that Happy Meal deal. It has a certain appeal!"

"Too late!" I bend my straw and blow a trickle of Coke at Bill. He retaliates by opening a pepper packet and flinging it at me.

That's when we go nuts.

Jeff grabs a ketchup packet while Meredith goes for the mustard. Bill and I scoop up handfuls of both. We're all laughing like crazy and squirting condiments all over each other while the customers and McDonald's workers gape at us like frozen guppies.

"Stop!" shouts the girl who served us, but then she gets hit with a splotch of mayo.

Two minutes later, we've given up and collapsed on the floor, still cracking up. We're covered in red and yellow glop and dripping with Coke. The floor tiles and walls around us are smeared and splattered even worse. We might have also flung a little mustard on a nearby toddler and her mom, but it could also have been pureed squash.

"What's going on here?" roars a man in a white shirt, polyester pants, and a Ronald McDonald tie

as he stomps over. He, of course, glares at *me*. Yes, somehow, Jacky Ha-Ha always looks like the ringleader when anything fun goes down.

"You and your friends need to vacate these premises. Now!"

"Okay, okay. We were just—"

"I know what you were doing, and you're never setting foot in here ever again." Then he stares at me, hard. "Do I know you?"

"Nope," I say, fast as I can. "Don't think so. Bye!" I herd my new friends toward the exit.

Because I recognize the McDonald's manager.

Two summers ago, he was a lifeguard. Working for my father.

Oops.

CHAPTER 27

That night, I write another letter to my mom.

I tell her how great things are going at play practice and how cool the theater kids all are. I do *not* mention Mrs. Turner's harebrained scheme about me standing up in public and making a speech. If I did, my mother would probably think I was making it up as a joke. After all, she's heard me stutter my whole life.

The next day at school, I have one of my special appointments with Ms. Alvarez. She's very nice. She's the school counselor.

Okay, she's a shrink. A psychologist.

Ever since last year, when I got in trouble on the first day of sixth grade for replacing all the presidential photos on the classroom calendar with teen magazine cut-outs of adorable Keanu Reeves, Johnny Depp, Joey from the New Kids on the Block (a terrible boy band I was obsessed with), and Will Smith from *Fresh Prince of Bel-Air,* she's been trying hard to get to the bottom of this whole Ha-Ha mystery.

"I see a noticeable drop in your rate of detentions," she starts.

"I'm having fun being in the play," I say.

"More fun than causing trouble in class?"

"I guess. Ms. O'Mara is pretty neat."

Ms. Alvarez nods. She also acts like she's waiting for me to say something else, so I do.

"Tickets go on sale next week. Teachers get a discount. Probably counselors, too. Of course, you probably shouldn't come to a performance when my family's there."

"Why not?"

"They'll take up half the seats."

She opens her folder and checks her notes. "You come from a large family, correct?"

"Well, no one is actually large. Hannah is what you might call pleasantly plump. She has a sweet tooth. Not sure which one it is. Probably a canine." I know I'm babbling, but I just can't stop the awful puns from spilling out. "Not that all canines are sweet. Old Mrs. Smilofsky up the street has the meanest Schnauzer I've ever met."

"Jacky, does everything have to be a joke with you?"

"Huh?"

"I get the sense that you feel a need to constantly be 'on.' To always be entertaining."

"You're not going to tell me to stop being funny, are you? Because Mrs. Bucci already worked that angle. 'Beware of wanting to be liked too much.' *Wooooo!* 'Beware the Ides of March.'"

"That's a line from *Julius Caesar*. I take it you like Shakespeare?"

"Never met the guy, but he seems okay. I'd like him better without the ruffled collar and all the rhymes."

"I understand that you and your friends like to rhyme. Especially at McDonald's."

Oh, boy. Somebody ratted us out.

"We were just having fun."

"Mrs. Jordan didn't find it amusing, and neither did the customers whose clothes you ruined and the workers who had to clean up your mess."

I think I gulp. Just like a cartoon. GULP!

"Was she there?"

Ms. Alvarez nods again. "Mrs. Jordan also told me that you skipped your meeting with her."

So Mrs. Jordan is the one who squealed on me?

I pretend I don't have a clue what Ms. Alvarez is talking about. I raise my eyebrows and do the sideways-head-tilt thing Sandfleas does when she's confused and can't tell whether I want her to sit, stay, or give me her paw.

"The Oratorical Contest." Ms. Alvarez hands me a slick brochure. "Apparently it's sponsored by the American Legion. There are contests all over the country. The first-place winner at the national finals takes home a very nice prize. There's an awards banquet...."

"I'm k-k-kind of busy with play practice."

"But, as evidenced by your recent antics at McDonald's, you still have an abundance of creative energy. Surely you can channel it in two directions simultaneously?"

"I don't know. You ever see a d-d-d-dog try to chase two squirrels at once? Its head and its butt kind of run in two different directions and snap back together like a r-r-rubber band. Ouch."

"So how are things at home?"

I slump in my chair. "Not great."

"How so?"

"Well, for one thing, my mom isn't there."

"Why not?"

"President Bush sent her to Saudi Arabia."

"Oh, I didn't know your mother was in the military. Operation Desert Shield?"

"That's the one." I see Ms. Alvarez is gobbling up my sob story, so I decide to toss her a few more tidbits. "Also, my oldest sister, Sydney, isn't living with us anymore, either."

"And where is she? Saudi Arabia?"

"Close. Princeton."

"Oh, I didn't realize your sister had gone away to college."

"Well, she did. Packed her bags and moved out. I know she had to, but it's been hard for—"

An alarm clock clangs its bell. "Sorry," says Ms. Alvarez. "Time's up."

I leave her office, possibly feeling even worse than when I walked in. The next time I need "psychiatric counseling," I think I'll talk to Meredith.

After all, she's playing Lucy in the show. And when Lucy opens her psychiatric help booth in the *Peanuts* comic strip, the doctor is always in.

Plus, she only charges a nickel.

CHAPTER 28

That Sunday, we go to church.

And we have to dress up for it. And by dress up, I mean we have to wear *dresses*. This is not something I like to do on a regular basis. You can't win a bike race in a dress. You can't climb a Ferris wheel in a dress. There is very little you can do in a dress unless you're Barbie; then you can have a Dream House *and* a Clothing Boutique.

Dad does a quick inspection in the living room and then we all pile into the family van, which is Mom's car when she's home.

Just being in it and seeing Mom's favorite Dunkin'

Donuts travel mug sitting in the cup holder makes me feel the need to talk to God about one very important topic: Him keeping an eye out for her.

We go to a Protestant church called St. Elizabeth's Chapel-by-the-Sea. It's not very crowded on most Sundays, only in the summer when tourists flock to Seaside Heights. The pastor, Reverend Zelley, always says a special prayer for Mom and all the other soldiers far from home, serving overseas in Operation Desert Shield.

I say my own prayer that God will do something to solve the Persian Gulf crisis before a single shot is fired in that desert. Sometimes I wonder if He might be the only one who can make a difference over there. Of course, I understand that God works through people, like He did with Ms. O'Mara standing up for Meredith. But if the people He has to work with (guys like Saddam Hussein) aren't paying attention to what He's telling them, there's not a whole lot He can do.

Before Mom deployed to Saudi Arabia, I used to spend my church time doodling on the Bible story coloring book pages they put in the pews to keep little kids quiet. I remember one Sunday when the illustration was "Jonah and the Whale." I gave it a new caption.

Then I colored the waterspout spewing out of the whale's blow- hole green and labeled it WHALE BOOGERS.

Now, with Mom so close to a serious combat situation, I'm too busy to goof around like that. I spend all of my pew time saying prayers for Mom and all the other moms, dads, brothers, sisters, sons, and daughters who are spending their Sundays far away from home, serving our country. I also say a prayer for Nonna. That's my mom's mom, my sweet Italian grandmother. It's been scary for her to have her daughter in a war zone on the other side of the world.

"Lord," I pray silently, "protect my mom the way she protects everybody else. Bless her and bring her home. I need her. We all do. But to be totally honest, I think I might need her a little more than everybody else."

CHAPTER 29

After church, I crawl out of my dress, pull on my jeans, and head down to the boardwalk to meet up with Meredith and Bill.

It's not an official rehearsal, but we've decided to help each other learn our lines.

Also, I think I maybe, possibly have a crush on Bill. I don't know for sure because I've never had a crush on anyone before. Plus, I don't want to end up like Hannah or Sophia and go totally boy-crazy.

But Bill does have very nice hazel eyes. And he's sweet. Funny, too.

He's also friendly, courteous, kind, obedient, cheerful, thrifty, brave, clean, and reverent.

No. Wait. That's the Boy Scouts.

feel free to color in Bill's eyeballs. They're kind of greenish brown and sparkly.

Anyway, since it's very late September, we practically have the boardwalk to ourselves. Most of the food stalls are closed up for the season. I, for one, am pretty happy about that. After our end-of-summer pig-out-and-puke, I'm really not in the mood for any more boardwalk grub.

Bill, Meredith, and I rehearse our first scene together—the lead-in to my song called "Snoopy."

"I think Snoopy's such a wonderful dog," says Meredith's character, Lucy.

"Me too," says Bill, as Charlie Brown. "He's just about the best there is."

When he says that line, he looks right at me with those big, hazel-colored eyeballs I mentioned earlier. I look at him. He looks at me some more. I look at him. Him, me. Me, him.

"Um, Jacky?" says Meredith.

"Yeah?"

"That's your cue."

"Oh. Right. Duh."

And, with Meredith tapping out the beat with her right foot, I sing the Snoopy song a cappella, which means without instruments, and should not be confused with singing "Acapulco," which sounds like a song about a beach in Mexico.

Singing Acapulco

The lyrics of the first verse remind me a little of what Mrs. Bucci said to me in English class. Maybe Snoopy's last name was Ha-Ha, too. He wants people to like him as much as I want people to like me. And, of course, he's surprised when they do.

We knock off our boardwalk rehearsal around four thirty. I hurry home because I don't want to be late for dinner. Meredith hurries home with me because she's hungry. Bill, unfortunately, already has dinner plans.

But, once again, dinner is delayed because Dad is working late.

"He has to work late? On a Sunday?" Meredith says it before I do.

"Apparently," I say, "lifeguards have a lot of paperwork this time of year."

"Paperwork? For what?"

"I'm not sure," I say. "He might be trying to sue all the jellyfish for physical and emotional anguish."

Meredith shivers. "Don't blame him. Those things are nasty."

"Why doesn't he come home at night?" grouses Riley.

"Maybe he doesn't like us anymore," says supersensitive Hannah.

"I'm sure he has a very mature, adult reason for his tardiness," says Victoria, "that none of you would understand."

"Well, I'm not asking him about it," I say.

No one argues.

They know if I confronted Dad it would come out like "Wh-wh-where w-w-were y-y-you..."

My first question would take three hours.

"Guess what, you guys?" says Sophia, changing the subject. "I broke up with Chad."

"The prepster?" I say.

"Yuh-huh. I'm back with Mike Guadagno. He's so nice."

"Yes," says Hannah, sighing sadly. "He's very nice."

"I'm hungry," says Emma, the Little Boss. She opens the emergency-cash cookie jar. "We have enough for one pie."

She picks up the phone and orders another pizza. Plain.

"No sausages, no pepperonis, no meatballs, no anchovies, no nothing," she tells the guy on the other end of the line. "Just plain cheese."

We each get a slice and a half for dinner.

Except for Dad. He doesn't come home until nearly midnight, and by then, the pizza's all gone.

CHAPTER 30

Nonna, my grandmother, isn't feeling so great.

"They called from the old folks' home," says Sophia on Monday. "Nonna is feeling queasy."

"It's probably the food they serve at that place," says Victoria. "Did you know..."

She goes on to tell us something none of us knew (or wanted to know) about the unsanitary kitchen conditions in many New Jersey nursing homes.

"We should go see her," I say,

because I really love my grandmother—and not just because she reminds me of her daughter, my mom.

"I can't," says Sophia. "Mike is supposed to call. I need to be by the phone when he does."

Yes, in 1990, you couldn't just slip a phone in your purse and take it with you. It was attached to the house and you had to sit and wait for it to ring.

"Dad will be home for dinner soon," says the ever-hopeful Hannah. "We sure don't want to miss that."

"There's probably nothing wrong with Nonna," says Sister Know-It-All Victoria. "She just wants attention."

As a middle child, I can relate.

Riley and I decide to bike over to Nonna's place to check on her.

"Tell Dad where we went," I tell Hannah. "Don't hold dinner for us."

On the way over to Nonna's rest home, I have an idea—one I know she'll love. I stop at a pay phone booth, drop in a quarter, and call Meredith. She says she'll call everybody else.

"Do they have a piano?" she asks.

"Yeah, in the parlor."

"Cool. I'll call Mr. Brimer, too."

Nonna's nursing home is a very nice, very old Victorian mansion. She has her own room upstairs, but she's waiting for us down in the parlor with five or six of her elderly friends. She beams when Riley and I bound through the doors.

"Hiya, Nonna!" I say, throwing out my arms wide like singers used to do in vaudeville.

"Hello, girls," she says, clapping her hands in delight.

"Are you feeling any better?" asks Riley.

"Eh," Nonna says with a shrug. "*Mezza mezza.* I've felt better, I've felt worse."

"Is there anything we can do for you?" asks Riley.

Nonna takes her hand. Pats it. "You're here, honey. That's enough. Jacky?"

"Yes, Nonna?"

She beams at me. "Make me laugh."

CHAPTER 31

There's a knock on the screen door.

Meredith, Bill, Dan, Jeff, Beth, Mr. Brimer, and Ms. O'Mara are out on the porch. I see Colleen, the techie, too. She's carrying a clip-on piano light.

"Is it okay if some friends help me?" I ask.

"Sure," says Nonna, rocking back in her chair with laughter. "The more the merrier."

"Come on in, guys."

Everybody piles into the parlor. Colleen organizes the furniture and wheelchairs into a half circle so Nonna and her friends can be our audience. Beth clips the portable work light onto the piano, then helps Mr. Brimer set up his sheet music.

"We thought we'd do the two numbers in the best shape," says Ms. O'Mara. "Meredith and Dan doing 'Schroeder.' You and Bill doing 'Suppertime.'"

I nod. Eagerly. I even pant a little, like Snoopy would. I'm getting into character.

When everything's set up and ready to go, I'm choking back a tear. I can't believe these guys dropped everything and came rushing over to help me make my grandmother smile.

"I d-d-don't know how to th-th-thank you guys."

"Uh-uh-uh," warns Ms. O'Mara. "I heard your grandmother. She wanted laughter, not tears."

"It's true," says Mr. Brimer. "I heard her, too."

He sits down at the piano and plinks out the opening notes of Beethoven's *Moonlight* Sonata. Dan

Napolitano is sitting cross-legged on the floor, pretending a coffee table is his toy piano. Meredith leans on it Lucy-style and launches into her Schroeder song.

Nonna and her friends are laughing so hard, tears are streaming down their cheeks.

And then Bill and I launch into our "Suppertime" number. I borrow a glass candy dish I see sitting on a doily and use it as my dog bowl.

We bring down the house.

I know opening night is still three weeks away and I know it will be extremely exciting when we're all in our costumes and performing on the set Mr. Foster is building for us. But to tell you the truth, I don't think the world premiere of *Charlie Brown*—at school or even on Broadway—could possibly feel as wonderful as doing those two numbers for my grandmother.

We made Nonna laugh.

Jacky Ha-Ha is happy.

CHAPTER 32

Late that night, I relive the whole glorious event and the smile on Nonna's face when I write all about it to Mom in another letter.

But then the sun rises. Time for school.

"Have you seen Mrs. Jordan?" Mrs. Turner asks me.

I try to buy some time. "I think so. She's the nice lady who teaches social studies, coaches the debate team, and eats at McDonald's, right? She's about yay tall..."

"Jacky." Mrs. Turner is giving me her look. Raised eyebrows are involved. "Mrs. Jordan is waiting for you. In her room. Now."

"Gee, I have—"

"A pass." She hands it to me. "This will let Mrs. Bollendorf know that you are late to biology because I sent you to see Mrs. Jordan."

"But we're dissecting worms today. Of course, I sort of wonder why. I mean, what's inside a worm? Dirt?"

"Jacky, there's no use trying to distract me. My mind is made up. You will be participating in the oratory contest or you will be suspended."

"F-f-for what?"

"Dereliction of duty. Willfully refusing to perform your duties and/or utilize your God-given talents."

"B-b-but—"

"No buts. The school play has been good for you.

The speech contest will be even better. Go. Mrs. Jordan is waiting."

I'm ready to burst into tears, but I don't really want to let Mrs. Turner know she can do that to me. So I fume and sputter instead. "A sp-sp-speech? D-d-do you r-r-really expect m-m-me to get up in f-f-front of p-p-people and sp-sp..." I'm so furious I can't even spit out a complete sentence. "S-see wha-wha-what you're do-do-doing to me?"

Mrs. Turner sighs. "Jacky," she whispers, "did you ever think that, maybe, studying public speaking could help you *speak in public?*"

And I finally get it.

This speech contest is another one of those "it'll be good for you" things. Like broccoli and literature (also known as boring books without pictures).

Read it. It will be good for you.

" ★★★★★ Five thousand hours of tasty reading." Betty Crocker

BROCCOLI BOOK

I slump down the hall to Mrs. Jordan's room, or, as I like to think of it, the lobby of hell.

"Good afternoon, Miss Hart," says Mrs. Jordan quite crisply when I enter her classroom. She's sitting—ramrod stiff—at her desk in the otherwise empty room. She's very prim and proper: buttons the top button of all her blouses, wears pearls. Seriously. *Pearls.*

"Hello," I mutter as I close the door behind me. I don't want anybody wandering the halls to pick up a juicy new piece of Jacky Ha-Ha gossip.

"I am given to understand that Assistant Principal Turner is very keen on your joining my oratorical team," says Mrs. Jordan.

"That makes one of us," I say under my breath as I study my shoelaces.

"Specifically," Mrs. Jordan continues with very clipped diction (you can hear every consonant), "Mrs. Turner suggests that you would do well in the local American Legion Oratorical Competition. In fact, she has so much faith in your rhetorical abilities, she even suggested that you might move on to the state round and, afterward, the national finals."

Something about her voice makes me look up from my shoes so I can study her face.

Well, whaddya know? From her extremely sour expression, I can tell: She's about as interested in me joining her speechifying team as I am.

"Well," I say, as cheerily as I can, "if you already have enough people..."

The door creaks open behind me. Someone else steps into the room.

"Nonsense," says this new person. "There's always room for one more."

I recognize the voice.

It's Ms. O'Mara.

CHAPTER 33

"Hello, Mrs. Jordan. I'm Katherine O'Mara."

"Yes?" says Mrs. Jordan, in the same tone the Queen of England would say, "We are not amused."

"I'm new in the English department, teaching the honors class and directing the fall play."

"So I have been told."

"Any idea about the assigned topics this year?"

"I beg your pardon?"

"The American Legion Oratorical Contest. The year I was in it, I gave my prepared oration on a citizen's duties, and then we had to talk for at least three minutes but no more than five about the Eighth

Amendment to the United States Constitution."

"Wait," I say. "Y-y-you had to make up a speech on the spot?"

Ms. O'Mara nods. "We all knew it would be on one of five constitutional topics given out beforehand so we could focus our research and prep. But then, yeah, right before the last prepared speech, they tell you the topic for your second speech. And boom—five minutes later you're on your feet talking about excessive bail or cruel and unusual punishment."

Cruel and unusual punishment is asking ME to be in a sp-sp-speech contest!

"Forgive my curiosity, Ms. O'Mara," says Mrs. Jordan, with the hint of a smirk. "How did you fare in the competition?"

"Pretty good. I won the local contest and was supposed to move on to the state round, but this Broadway thing opened up..."

"'This Broadway thing'?" Mrs. Jordan crinkles her nose like somebody just fried fish in her classroom.

Ms. O'Mara waves it off. "This was a long time ago. I was just a little older than Jacky. I could sing and dance some, so they put me in *Annie*."

"They did?" says Mrs. Jordan, finally sounding slightly impressed.

Ms. O'Mara nods. "I played Tessie. The crybaby orphan." She slips into a cutesy-poo baby doll voice and says, "'Oh my goodness!'"

"That was you?"

"A very young me. Anyway, I couldn't go to the state competition. But when I went to teachers college, I did minor in speech and theater."

She turns to me when she says that last part.

And I get the point. The two are linked. Hey, you really can't do theater without getting up in front of people and saying stuff—also known as making a speech.

Ms. O'Mara smiles at Mrs. Jordan. "I'd like to help you coach the team this year."

"No need. I don't require a helper."

"I know how time-consuming it can be, with all the prep and practice."

"Fine," says Mrs. Jordan. "You can coach *her*." She flaps her flipper at me. "I'm certain Mrs. Turner will be thrilled to hear of your involvement."

"Great. What do you say, Jacky? We can work on your prepared speech in between rehearsals for *Charlie Brown*. And I'll help you organize your research for the second speech, too."

I'm all set to protest, but I realize this really isn't my day to get my way. So I surrender.

"F-f-fine."

Mrs. Jordan shakes her head dismissively. "Good luck, Ms. O'Mara. I have a feeling you're going to need it. By the way, while you were in college, did you take any courses related to speech therapy? If so, perhaps you can help Jacky overcome her very unfortunate speech impediment."

me when somebody says I have a
SPEECH IMPEDIMENT

My burning-red ears betray me. Ms. O'Mara can tell I'm about to go ballistic. But before I can, she grabs me by the elbow and guides me out the door.

"Thanks, Mrs. Jordan."

When we're safely down the hall, Ms. O'Mara tells me, "Critics. When you're a performer, you have to learn to ignore them, Jacky. Especially the dumb ones, and there's a lot of them. You can spot them when they say or write something completely idiotic."

I put on a snooty snob voice and clip my diction.

"Oh? You mean critics such as Mrs. Jordan?"

"Sorry. Don't know who you're talking about."

"You're ignoring her already, right?"

"Yep. See how easy it is?"

CHAPTER 34

That afternoon, right after play practice, when we're all hanging out in the auditorium, I ask Ms. O'Mara about the part of the American Legion Oratorical Contest that's freaking me out the most.

"So, did you really have to make up a speech, right on the spot?"

"Yep. The contest is done in two parts. First you give your prepared speech."

"Which you can read off a sheet of paper, right?"

Ms. O'Mara shakes her head. "Nope. But it's just like memorizing your lines for this show, Jacky. You write down what you want to say and practice it every chance you get. Before long, you've memorized it."

"But how do you do that second speech?" asks Meredith.

"First," says Ms. O'Mara, "you do your homework on the five topics the judges can choose from."

"And then what?" asks Bill.

Yes, the whole cast is interested, because if they were in my shoes, they'd be terrified, too. This makes me feel better.

"You build a speech with the blocks of what you know," says Ms. O'Mara. "It's a lot like doing improv in theater."

"So, when you improvise a scene, you just wing it?" I ask.

JACKY'S SHOES

"Not exactly." She looks around mysteriously like she's about to let us in on a big secret. "There is a hidden structure to improv. You say 'yes, and' to whatever comes along. You take what you're given and add to it—you never say no. You never deny. For instance, let's say Meredith and I are improvising a scene. Come on, Meredith."

Ms. O'Mara climbs up onstage. Meredith scampers up the steps to join her.

"Okay, I'll start," Ms. O'Mara says. "Wow! It sure is cold in here."

"Actually," says Meredith, "I think it's kind of warm."

Ms. O'Mara makes a rude buzzer noise. "Sorry. Wrong answer. You denied my setup."

"But the radiators always make this room too hot...."

"You're supposed to be acting, Meredith," says Dan Napolitano, very kindly. "You know—welcome to the world of make-believe."

"Oh. Okay. Let's try again."

Ms. O'Mara pretends like she's shivering. "Wow. It sure is cold in here."

"See?" says Meredith. "I told you we shouldn't have crawled into this ice chest."

"But I wanted to skate across the ice cubes," says Ms. O'Mara, picking up on what Meredith laid down. "That's why we took those shrinking pills."

"Oops," says Meredith. "Mine is wearing off."

She starts acting like her arms are expanding, like she's inflating.

"Careful!" cries Ms. O'Mara in a high-pitched helium-sucking voice. "I'm still soooo tiny."

Meredith looks at her foot. "Uh-oh. Sorry. Didn't mean to step on you."

"And...scene!" cries Ms. O'Mara.

She and Meredith take a little bow while the rest of us crack up and give them a standing ovation.

How to do something wonderful, right away

And that's how I learned how to write sketches for *Saturday Night Live*. It all started with skating on ice cubes.

CHAPTER 35

Early Saturday morning, when our chores are finished, I dash off a quick letter to Mom. I teach her how to do improv, just in case she and some of the other marines want to start a Desert Shield comedy troupe! Then Riley and I decide we want to head down to the boardwalk for swirl cones.

We go to tell Dad what we're up to and he's nowhere to be found.

"So do you think he had to work again?" asks Riley.

And, practicing my own newly acquired improvisational skills, I say, "Yes. I think there might be a New Jersey state lifeguard convention in town this weekend."

We hike up the steps to the boardwalk.

"A lifeguard convention?" says Riley.

"Oh, yes," I tell her. "They need to vote on next year's swim trunks. I think Dad's all about keeping them red and baggy, but there are a few lifeguards, mostly from the Atlantic City area, who are pushing for polka-dot Speedos."

I'm all set to keep *yes and*-ing when I see Dad.

He's at this pizza place, sitting on a stool, sharing a slice and yukking it up with Jenny Cornwall, the prettiest girl on the beach.

I nudge Riley and we hide behind a Wheel of Fortune near a booth filled with pink and blue teddy bears.

"Is that pretty lifeguard girl going to the convention, too?" whispers Riley.

"No," I say, breaking all my new improv rules. "They won't let her in. She's nothing but trouble."

"What do you mean?"

"Never mind. You're too young to know."

"I am not—"

"They're going somewhere!" I see Dad crumple up his paper plate and toss it into a trash barrel. Jenny Cornwall grabs her Coke cup. The two of them stroll down the boardwalk.

They're not holding hands, but when they swing their arms back and forth, their fingers come dangerously close to brushing each other.

Riley and I follow behind them, using phone booths, T-shirt mounds, gigantic stuffed dolls, and racks of inflatable beach toys for cover.

194

I see Dad glance at his dive watch. He says something to Jenny.

They pick up their pace.

So do we.

Well, I do. Riley bumps into one of those mountains of T-shirts. Knocks the whole table over. We lose valuable time picking everything up so the skeevy guy running the tourist trap doesn't have us arrested for vandalizing his vast collection of I'M WITH STUPID clothing.

When we're done refolding and restacking the shirts, we've totally lost Dad.

Then I see a red convertible speeding out of a parking slot near the boardwalk. Jenny Cornwall, hair blowing in the breeze like she's starring in a shampoo commercial, is behind the wheel.

And Dad's in the passenger seat.

CHAPTER 36

Riley and I head for home, neither one of us saying a word.

We never do buy swirl cones.

Riley's sniffling some. Even though we both feel incredibly betrayed by our father, she lets her emotions show more than me. Because I'm Jacky Ha-Ha.

And no one likes a sad clown.

Fortunately, when we get home, Sydney is there!

That's right, my oldest sister. The one who goes to Princeton, which, in case you didn't know, is a big-deal Ivy League school. That means, when it comes to ivy vines crawling up the sides of old buildings, it's one of the top schools in the whole country. Right up there with vine-tangled Harvard, Yale, and Brown, which, if you ask me, is a pretty dull name for a college. What were the other options for the school's name? Tan? Beige?

Dad, of course, isn't home, seeing how he and Jenny just took off in her super-cool convertible. But everybody else is. All my sisters are thrilled to see Sydney. Even Sophia, who doesn't mind temporarily relinquishing her crown as the "oldest sister currently at home."

I notice that Sydney has several suitcases, a couple of boxes filled with books, and a very large duffel bag—even though I'm assuming she's only home for a day or two because she has class first thing Monday morning.

"Planning on doing a lot of reading and laundry this weekend?" I ask.

And, instantly, Sydney starts bawling her eyes out. Not exactly the reaction I was going for.

"I'm flunking out!" she blubbers through her torrent of tears.

At least, I think that's what she said. When people are simultaneously crying and talking, it's sometimes hard to understand what they're trying to say. It comes out, "I-I-I, I-I-I, amb fa-huh-huh-lunk-k-k-ing ow-ow-out!"

"That's impossible," I say. "You're super-smart."

"You're the smartest one of all of us," says Victoria, our resident know-it-all. "Well, at least until I take my SATs..."

"What do you need to feel better?" asks Hannah. "How about fudge? Would fudge work? Because I have some peanut butter swirl in the fridge."

"I could order a pizza," says Emma. "I'll even tell them to put pepperoni on it."

"That's still your favorite, right?" asks Riley.

Sydney cracks a small smile, finds a tissue, and wipes away her tears.

"You guys are the best."

"So," I say, "what exactly should we tell Dad?"

Panic fills Sydney's eyes. "How about nothing?"

"Nothing works for me." I turn to my sisters. "You guys?"

They all nod. Except, of course, Victoria.

"Victoria?" I say.

"Well, if you ask me, it's very important for parents to—"

"Victoria?" I give her a look. The one Mrs. Turner gives me.

"Fine," she says. "We don't mention this to Dad. For now."

Sydney smiles. "Thanks, you guys."

Dad comes home around six. He's incredibly thrilled to see Sydney, too. Can't blame him. As the oldest and most responsible kid, she's probably a breath of fresh air for him after having to deal with me.

Later that night, after everyone's in bed, I wake up and head down the hall to the bathroom.

I hear sobbing.

It's coming from the room Sydney shares with Sophia and Victoria, but I can tell Sydney is the one weeping. It's a sister thing. We recognize the sounds of each other's tears.

I tiptoe into the room.

Sydney's in her old bed near the window. Sobbing into her pillow.

"Are you okay?" I whisper.

"I've ruined my life, Jacky."

"No, you haven't. This is a just a bump in the road."

"More like a pothole."

"Well," I say, climbing into bed next to Sydney and spooning her, "they can fix potholes. You just need to pour in hot asphalt. It's stinky, what with all that smoldering tar and chunky asphalt gunk, but it works. Of course, pothole repairs always back up traffic, so don't be surprised when everybody starts honking their horns and shouting, 'Get out of the street, lady!' But you'll just say, 'Sorry, can't right now. Need to smooth out this bump in my road....'"

I keep spinning my silly story. Sydney is half-laughing, half-crying.

But she's drifting off. I lower my voice and keep going.

"Of course, they say the road to Princeton is paved with potholes. And dips. Lots and lots of dips. I've met a few alumni..."

When I hear my big sister's regular, steady breathing beside me, I finally stop.

I roll over and stare up at the ceiling.

And then (please don't tell anybody), I cry myself to sleep.

CHAPTER 37

Sunday's actually a fun day.

After church (and many silent prayers for Mom, Nonna, *and* Sydney), we go to the Sand Dollar Pancake House to celebrate Sydney being home. I devour a stack of cinnamon-crusted flapjacks. Sydney goes for the Nutella French toast, which, she says, "is to die for."

After brunch, Dad asks Sydney when she's heading back to Princeton.

"Not tonight" is all she says in reply.

"Don't you have classes tomorrow?"

"No," says Sydney. "It's Columbus Day."

"Then how come we have school?" moans Riley.

"Because," I say, "Christopher Columbus didn't discover New Jersey."

"Princeton is in New Jersey," says Victoria. "In fact, the school's original name was the College of New Jersey, but they changed it in 1896..."

And off she goes! While the rest of us wolf down our pancakes, guzzle orange juice, and chomp bacon, Victoria tells us everything we never wanted to know about Princeton.

At least her babbling lets Sydney off the hook. She doesn't have to tell Dad that the real reason she's not going back to her very expensive college is because she's flunking out.

How can Sydney afford to go to an Ivy League university on a lifeguard and soldier's salary? Easy. Our practically perfect big sister won a ton of scholarships. I guess she'll lose all that money now that her grades are in the toilet.

Dad leaves for work (or wherever) earlier than usual on Monday morning—before any of us are even out the door to school. Sydney is moping around the kitchen. Sighing a lot. Stirring her coffee without drinking a drop.

"So, Sydney?" I ask.

"Yeah?"

"What do you say we hit AC?"

"Atlantic City? Don't you have school?"

"I'm declaring a holiday. Come on. It'll be fun."

"I don't know...."

"We don't have to go into any of the casinos for entertainment. There are all sorts of performers working the boardwalk for spare change. Magicians and jugglers and mimes."

I can tell Sydney's thinking about it. Sort of.

"There's a New Jersey Transit bus in fifteen minutes," I add.

Riley tugs on my sleeve. "We're supposed to go to school...."

"Can't. I'm not feeling good."

"You're not?" says Riley.

"Nope. And neither are you. That's why Sydney is calling the school office to let them know she's keeping us home today."

Sydney looks surprised. "I am?"

"Your voice sounds the most grown-up-ish. Tell them you're our aunt and you're here looking after us while Mom serves her country over in the Middle East and Dad guards lives on the beach."

206

Sydney hesitates until I start doing a countdown to bus departure time.

"Ten minutes. Nine minutes and fifty-five seconds..."

"All right, already!"

Riley and I are, officially, skipping school to hang with our big sister.

Hello, this is Jacqueline and Riley Hart's aunt. My name? Auntie Mame...

So much for solemn vows made on the top of Ferris wheels.

Jacky Ha-Ha is back.

And she's not leaving until she sees her big sister smile.

CHAPTER 38

After a three-hour-and-twenty-minute bus ride, my two sisters and I are ready to hit the Atlantic City boardwalk.

Right after we find an Atlantic City bathroom.

I can't believe that Sydney actually went along with this whole wacky idea. It's so *not* Sydney that it's perfect. Which means it *is* very Sydney after all. Someone will probably give her another scholarship for excellence in aunt impersonation.

If *I* get caught, though, Mrs. Turner will probably come up with something else "good" for me to do. Maybe she'll make me run for class president. All the candidates have to make sp-sp-speeches, too.

I am, however, glad that there's no *Charlie Brown* rehearsal until tomorrow. I wouldn't want to let the gang down. Or Ms. O'Mara. Wow. Maybe I am mellowing out.

Or not.

Because the instant I see the buskers (that's what they call street performers) on the boardwalk, I want to join in.

There's a magician who does sleight of hand and card tricks with a bunny rabbit. A lady named Fannie clapping and singing gospel songs. Up near Ventnor Avenue, we see jugglers and a guy on stilts and one of those mechanical men, his face painted silver, who only goes into his robot moves after people drop money in his open cigar box.

All of these "street" performers have some kind of container for folks to toss money into.

"Good thing I brought my lunch box," I say.

I give Riley my sandwich and apple.

"What are you doing?" asks Sydney.

"It's showtime."

I prop the lunch box open on the boardwalk, back up against the railing, and motion for Sydney and Riley to move to the sides of my stage.

"Please don't sing that Snoopy song again," says Riley.

"Don't worry. I'm not singing. I'm improvising."

What I start doing is kind of wild. I just play off whatever happens around me. For instance, a flock of seagulls dive-bombs Riley, going for my bologna and cheese sandwich.

"Step right up, folks, and see a live remake of *The Birds,* the classic Hitchcock horror movie about our feathered friends becoming bloodthirsty killers!"

A guy walks by wearing a backpack.

I walk alongside him. "It's okay, sir. You can take off the parachute. You're on the ground."

I'm attracting a crowd. It's small, but it's growing.

When I have a pretty big crowd, I change my mind. I grab somebody's popcorn box and, using it as my dog food bowl, I launch into "Suppertime" from the show.

Pretty soon, my lunch box is half full. And it's not just coins. Some people are dropping in paper money. One guy (who must've done pretty well at the casinos) slips in a fifty!

When a sweet lady asks me how much she should give, I say, "Take five out of your wallet and give me the rest."

At least she laughs.

In fact, a lot of people are laughing.

I realize, *Hey, maybe I could make a living like this.*

"You're the best, Jacky!" says Sydney when my show is finished.

"So are you," I say. "No, wait, Riley's the best."

"Thanks!" says Riley.

"Wait a second," I say. "We're all the best. All the Hart girls, including Mom."

"We're awesome," says Sydney.

"In fact," I add, "some of us are practically perfect."

I see a couple strolling by holding hands. "How'd you guys like to hear a great joke for a quarter? It's about this couple I met on the boardwalk in Atlantic City. Looked just like you two..."

Thirty minutes and a dozen jokes later, we have more than enough money for a humongous lunch and the bus ride home.

We also have a much happier big sister.

CHAPTER 39

On the ride home to Seaside Heights, Sydney tells us the awful, unforgivable truth: She got a C+ on an English paper.

You heard that right. In her "practically perfect" world, a C+ on one paper equals completely flunking out of college.

"Guess I overreacted, huh?"

"Little bit," I say.

"Well, I'm heading back to Princeton tomorrow."

"So, you didn't miss a single class?"

"Nope. My attendance record is still perfect."

"Just like you!"

And then I hug her. And then Riley hugs me. And then Sydney hugs Riley. Yes, it's a wild and crazy hug-fest in the last row of that northbound New Jersey Transit bus.

We get home a little late and, since Dad isn't there (what else is new?), Emma orders everybody another pizza. Plain cheese, of course.

We settle down with our slices in front of the TV set because Monday night at eight on the Buy a Bargain Channel is when Crazy Colonel Davies is on.

He runs a call-in show where you can buy all sorts of weird and wacky faux antiques. (*Faux* is another word for "fake.")

"Call him up, Jacky!" says Riley, my number one cheerleader.

I pick up the phone and punch in the 800 number.

"Did you get through?" asks Victoria. "Because the best way to get through to a radio or TV show is to—"

"I'm in," I tell her.

"Oh. Then never mind."

My other sisters applaud. They love when I go one-on-one with Colonel Davies.

"This is going to be a hoot!" says Hannah.

"Why?" asks Sydney, because she's not home on Monday nights anymore. "What's Jacky going to do?"

"You'll see," says Sophia. "It's very immature. But it's also hysterical."

"It's funny, too," adds Emma.

On the screen, Colonel Davies is holding what he calls an "antique" sterling silver ring.

"Your friends will wonder which one of your relatives died and left it to you," says Colonel Davies as he shows off the ring. "But don't worry. We won't tell them your secret. And it's only nineteen ninety-five! Okay, I see our phone lines are lighting up already. Hello, caller?"

And I'm on.

"Hello, Colonel Davies," I say in the warbly voice of a cartoon granny. You know, the one who owns Tweety Bird. "My name is Amanda Hugginkiss."

"Hello, Amanda," says the colonel. He holds up the ring with his free hand. "Like what you see?"

"Well, Colonel, that's just it. I lost my glasses. All I can see is a blur and a blob. You're the blob. The ring is a blur. A teeny, tiny blur."

My six sisters have their hands over their mouths so they don't laugh out loud and ruin my gag.

"Well, let me describe this absolutely beautiful antique—"

"Who are you calling an antique, you young whippersnapper?"

"Not you, Amanda. This beautiful ring, on the other hand..."

"You have another ring on your other hand?"

"Okay, Amanda, maybe we should—"

"It's Amanda *Hugginkiss*," I snap at him. "If you ever need me, just say 'I'm looking for Amanda Hugginkiss.'"

And then I start howling at the moon like I did on top of the Ferris wheel.

Colonel Davies starts seething.

"Oh, it's *you* again. The howler."

"*Aaaaa-oooooooo!*"

I'm Smiling so I don't Scream

Bargain Channel

Antique Silver ring almost FREE Shipping* (*$3.99)

only 19.95$

"Look here, little girl," he snarls into the phone. "We're tracing this call. The police will be dropping by later to speak with your parents!"

I slam the phone back into its cradle.

On the TV, Colonel Davies slams his phone down, too, and mutters, "I hate that kid."

Then he realizes he's still on TV. Live.

"But I love a bargain." He gives the camera his cheesiest smile yet.

My sisters all crack up. Except sweet Hannah. She looks worried.

"Oh, no!" she says. "Do you think the police are really coming over here to arrest Jacky?"

"They'd better not," says Emma, balling up her fists.

"We won't let them in the door," says Victoria. "Unless they have a duly authorized warrant, signed by a judge..."

Yep. Thar she blows. Victoria gives us a five-minute lecture on our rights under the US Constitution, a talk I should probably pay attention to, since I'm supposed to be talking about the Constitution in my American Legion Speech-a-thon.

But I'm too busy smiling at Sydney, who's smiling at me.

"Thanks, Jacky," she says. "That's definitely the best show I've seen on TV all year."

Mission accomplished. I've cheered up my big sister. It's just what Jacky Ha-Ha does.

And someday, I promise, I'll do something nice for Colonel Davies to make up for all my crank calls.

But tonight was just for Sydney.

CHAPTER 40

The next morning, Sydney is gone before I'm even awake.

"A friend gave her a ride back to school," Hannah tells me. "A *guy* friend." She wiggles her eyebrows a lot when she says that bit.

Riley and I head back to school, too.

"How are you feeling?" asks Ms. O'Mara when I bump into her in the hall.

"Oh, much better, thank you," I say, making my voice sound as puny as possible. "I stopped throwing up around three o'clock. Yesterday afternoon. Not this morning. All we're eating are soft-boiled eggs and Wonder Bread."

"Jacky?"

"Yes?"

"Are you forgetting that I have a degree in speech and theater?"

"No."

"Good. Then you know I have been trained to recognize bad acting when I see it."

"B-b-but—"

She hands me a sheet of paper. "Here are the five

topics you need to know inside out for your extemporaneous speech."

"Thanks. I think."

"And I'll be happy to look over your prepared speech this afternoon, right after play practice."

"Um, I don't know if it'll be done by then."

"Make sure it is. And Jacky?"

"Yes, Ms. O'Mara?"

"Today's Tuesday. The whole cast is supposed to be off book."

"That means we need to have all our lines memorized, right?"

"Correct."

I was afraid that was what it meant.

I spent most of the weekend focused on taking care of my big sister instead of myself. So, needless to say, play practice isn't much fun that afternoon.

I say "Line" all the time, which is what you do when you can't remember what your line is and you want Colleen, who's reading along in the script, to tell you what you're supposed to say next. I say "Line" so many times you'd think Snoopy was a judge at a tennis tournament.

After rehearsal, everybody is shooting me dirty looks. But none of them are as nasty as the look on Ms. O'Mara's face when I hand her the prepared speech for the oratorical contest, which I wrote during lunch.

"I don't think the judges are looking for a four-word oration on the duties and obligations of a citizen under the Constitution of the United States."

"So, 'Be sure to vote' isn't enough? Even if I repeat it a few times?"

Ms. O'Mara actually sighs at me. "Jacky, since

we're on the subject of duties and obligations..."

Oh, boy. She's squinting at me the way people do when they peel back the bread on their sandwich and see something gross inside.

"You're letting the rest of the cast down," she says. "Being in a play is just like being on your Little League baseball team. Everybody else on that stage is counting on you to be at your best. How can *they* be great if you're not taking your part seriously? Will anybody in the audience remember Meredith's amazing voice or Bill's incredible comic timing if you're out there on opening night calling 'Line' every time you forget what you're supposed to say?"

"I'm sorry," I say. "It's just that—"

Ms. O'Mara puts up her hand to stop me.

"I'm not really interested in excuses, Jacky. Go home and write a better speech. Memorize the rest of Snoopy's lines and lyrics."

"I will," I say. "I promise."

"Good. Because if you don't..."

"What? You'd kick me out of the show?"

"What happens next is up to you, Jacky. Just like it always is."

CHAPTER 41

A nd so I embark on what I plan to be an all-nighter
(the first of many in my career, I might add).

I write a much better speech. It actually has a
beginning, a middle, and an end. I also open with a
joke. I read somewhere that opening with a joke is
a smart thing to do when you give a speech.

Next, I go to work memorizing Snoopy's speeches
from the play.

I walk around the house mumbling the monologue about being a World War One flying ace and
battling the Red Baron.

"'Curse you, Red Baron! Curse you and your kind!

Curse the evil that causes all this unhappiness.'"

During dinner (cheese pizza once again—Dad's not home) I say "Curse you, Red Baron!" to the shaker can of Parmesan cheese. After dinner, I say "Curse you, Red Baron!" to the dirty dishes soaking in the sink. When it's time to walk Sandfleas, I treat her to every single speech Snoopy makes in the show. I sing her every song. Sandfleas is a good audience. Mostly because it's garbage night and there's all sorts of trash cans and black plastic bags for her to sniff along the sidewalks.

We make it through all my lines and lyrics without me once shouting, or even thinking, "Line!"

"So, Sandfleas, Snoopy's a World War One flying ace. But what kind of hero would you be?"

The dog keeps on sniffing trash. She's used to me making up goofy stories about her on our last walk of the day.

"How about an astronaut? Sure, the Soviet Union sent all sorts of dogs into space. But they just went up and down or orbited the earth in a capsule. Commander Sandfleas is the first astronaut dog to ever venture outside the spaceship with nothing but a leash. Sandfleas takes the first dog walk in outer space. She also pees on a passing asteroid. And then, with one paw, she fixes the mirror on the Hubble Space Telescope!"

"So, you want to hear all of *Charlie Brown* again?" I ask Sandfleas as we come up the block toward our house. "We could do a double walk, it's so nice out tonight."

She wags her tail. Because our next-door neighbors have a crumpled chicken bucket, filled with chicken bones, sitting in their open trash bin. While Sandfleas examines the goodies, I glance up the street.

A little red convertible pulls into our driveway.

There's a woman behind the wheel.

Dad climbs out of the passenger seat.

"See you tomorrow, Jenny," I hear Dad say.

Because the driver is Jenny Cornwall, the prettiest girl on the beach.

"Curse you, Red Baron," I whisper. "Curse you and your kind. Curse the evil that causes all this unhappiness."

Sandfleas is staring up the street with me. She starts whimpering when Jenny Cornwall's sporty little convertible backs out of our driveway and swings up the street.

Dad's actually whistling as he bounds up the front steps. Guess he and Jenny had another amazing date. How many does that make this week? Does he really need to hang out with her every single night?

I can't believe he's doing this to us.

Worse, I can't believe he's doing it to Mom.

"Let's go home," I mutter to Sandfleas. "I need to write a letter."

CHAPTER 42

I don't even say hi to Dad when I come into the house.

    I go straight to my room and yank a clean sheet of paper out of my desk.

Dear Mom,

Hi! I hope you are safe and having a good week, because I am having the absolutely WORST week of my whole, entire life.

First of all, Sydney shows up and tells us she's flunking out of college so I drop everything to entertain her and make her smile because I think, sometimes, I love my sisters too much.

Then it turns out she's not really flunking out—she just got a C-plus on one paper. A C-plus! That means she's a little better than average, which, if you ask me, should be fine with anybody.

And, because of all the time I spent cheering up Sydney, the one teacher at school I sort of like, Ms. O'Mara, definitely doesn't like me anymore. She's the director of the school play and I didn't have my lines in the *You're a Good Man, Charlie Brown* script memorized on the day I was supposed to have them memorized. Also, I tried to joke my way through the first draft of this stupid American Legion speech I have to give because Mrs. Turner thinks it'll magically cure my stutter.

Ms. O'Mara is helping me on the speech

thing, too, and when she read what I wrote, I think she realized she's been wasting her time caring about me. I'm not Jacky Ha-Ha. I'm Jacky Hopeless.

But all of this is nothing compared to what Dad's been up to while you've been away from home. First of all, he's never here. He says he's "working." Seriously? How much work is there for a lifeguard—even the head lifeguard—in the middle of October? Do his duties include protecting trick-or-treaters on Halloween? Dad is never home for dinner, so all we ever eat nowadays is cheese pizza because Emma does the ordering. I'm thinking of changing my name to Jacky Cheeseball.

And the real reason Dad isn't ever home at night?

Brace yourself, Mom. And put down any

weapons or grenades you might have in your hands.

Because I'm pretty sure Dad has a new girlfriend. Jenny Cornwall. You remember her,... blond, body like a Barbie doll, lifeguards with Dad (which gives her an excuse to wear nothing but a swimsuit all day, every day). Ms. Cornwall is also known here in Seaside as the prettiest girl on the beach.

Anyway, if I were you, I'd go tell your general and President Bush that you can't stay in Saudi Arabia any longer. Forget Saddam Hussein, you need to come home and take care of us. And Dad. Before it's too late!

I write my letter in a blinding blaze of fury.
And then I go back and reread it.
Yowzer.
No way can I send *that* to Mom. So I fold it up, seal it in an envelope, and tuck it into a drawer.

Then I write another letter. Like all the others I send, it's all very Ha-Ha.

My second letter is all about how cute Emma is when she insists we only eat plain pizza. How great it was to see Sydney, who came home from Princeton for the long Columbus Day weekend. How hard Dad is working to take good care of us. How much I'm praying for Mom in church. How Nonna is doing better. How Sandfleas is the cutest dog in the whole world (I even add in a quick doggy doodle). Finally, I write two or three paragraphs about how much fun I'm having "starring" in the school play and working on a speech about every American citizen's duty.

When I'm finished writing the happy letter, I doodle some smiley faces all over the envelope. As I'm sealing it up, car headlights swing across my bedroom window. Somebody else just pulled into our driveway.

I peek through the curtains and see Sophia in the front seat of Mike Guadagno's car.

I'm glad they're back together. Hannah will be glad, too. Now she can be heartbroken about Mike at close range.

Not knowing I'm spying on her, Sophia leans over and kisses Mike. On the cheek.

I smile.

That kiss is a nice way to end an otherwise miserable day.

CHAPTER 43

Well done, everybody," says Ms. O'Mara when we finish rehearsal on Wednesday afternoon.

We all applaud each other.

"And special congratulations to Jacky Hart, who, somehow, managed to memorize her entire part in one night!"

More applause and *woo-hoos* from the cast.

While I'm packing up my stuff, Ms. O'Mara reads the revised speech I wrote.

"This is excellent," she says when she finishes.

"Thanks," I say. "See you tomorrow."

Okay, can I let you in on a little secret? As nice as Ms. O'Mara was to me, there was a little devil inside me that didn't think I deserved such good treatment.

Back then, when people tried to get close to me, my instinct was to push them away. Hard.

It's like when a private club in Beverly Hills allowed the famous comedian Groucho Marx to join. He immediately sent them a telegram saying, "Please accept my resignation. I don't want to belong to any club that will accept people like me as a member."

So, on our walk home with Bill and Meredith, my little devil and I have an awful idea.

"You guys thirsty?" I ask when we're on the sidewalk outside the 7-Eleven.

"I could go for a Slurpee or something," says Bill.

"I'm good," says Meredith. (Later, she'll be glad she said that.)

"My treat, Bill," I say.

"Nah, I've got it—"

"I insist. After all, I made you guys wait a whole extra day for me to get off book."

"It wasn't that big of a deal."

I show him the palm of my hand. The way Ms. O'Mara showed me hers.

"What flavor?" I ask.

"Cherry, if they've got it."

"One cherry Slurpee coming right up. Wait here."

I dash into the store and grab an empty Slurpee cup. Then, ignoring the funny looks from other customers, I go over to where they keep the condiments for the ancient hot dogs rolling around in the warmer. I pump some mustard and pickle relish into the bottom of my plastic cup. Then I tear open a couple of salt and pepper packets and sprinkle them on top of the hot dog goop. Finally, I go over to the

Slurpee machine, pull back the handle, and bury that foul-tasting gunk under a bright red slush pile with a frosty curlicue swirl on top.

I pop in a straw, make sure it sinks all the way down to the mustardy bottom, pay for the drink, and head outside, ready to deliver my best prank ever.

"Here you go, Bill."

"Thanks!"

He sucks on the straw.

The look on his face is hysterical.

Well, to *me,* anyway.

Bill starts gacking.

"What the heck is this?" he asks as he chokes.

"A new flavor: Cherry Mustard Pickle Pepper."

"Jacky?" says Meredith. "Is this another one of your stupid stunts?"

"Hey, they have a free fixin's bar," I say. "Why should people with hot dogs be the only ones who get to use it?"

I'm laughing.

They're not.

Meredith grabs Bill by the arm and hustles him into the convenience store.

"Come on," she says. "You need a bottle of water." Then she turns to me. "And you need to get your act together, Jacky."

Wow. My best friend, Meredith, sounds exactly like Ms. O'Mara.

Good, says the little devil in my head. *We're better off without them.*

And so we walk home.

Alone.

Just me and my little devil.

CHAPTER 44

I think about confessing my stupid Slurpee stunt to Mom in a letter. Do I like Bill Phillips so much that I'm trying to scare him away? Maybe Mom and I need to have a transatlantic mother-daughter chat courtesy of the United States Postal Service.

But the instant my pen touches paper, I remember: She's in Saudi Arabia waiting to go to war. She doesn't need to hear about the dumb pranks her immature middle child is pulling back home.

Maybe it's a good thing that, the very next day, I have another session with the school shrink, Ms. Alvarez.

I tell her about Sydney and Princeton.

"Is that what's bothering you?" she asks.

"Maybe. Probably. I guess."

Or maybe it's my dad constantly hanging out with the prettiest girl on the beach....

Or my mom being over in Saudi Arabia, where a full-blown war could explode any second.

Or me being a jerk to anybody who actually wants to be my friend.

Or my fear of letting down the one teacher whose opinion I really care about.

244

Or maybe what's really bothering me is the stupid nickname I just can't shake, the one that's been with me since kindergarten, when I first started stuttering in front of strangers, the one that tells me I'd better be funny at all times, no matter the cost, or else people will see who I really am.

But I don't tell Ms. Alvarez any of that.

So maybe it's not her fault that she's absolutely no help.

She's glancing at her battery-powered alarm clock, about to tell me that our time is up, when someone knocks on the door.

It's Mrs. Turner.

"Jacky?" she says. "You need to go to the hospital right now. It's your grandmother. Your family will meet you there."

From the look on Mrs. Turner's face I can tell: This is bad.

Really, really bad.

She hands me a slip of paper. Guess it's my Get Out of School Free card, good for one day only.

I hop on Le Bike and pedal over to the hospital.

The whole ride, I'm thinking, *How did that happen so fast?* It was just a few days ago that me and my friends (who maybe aren't my friends anymore) were entertaining Nonna and *her* friends at the rest home.

I'm the first one to arrive at Nonna's hospital room.

She's hooked up to all sorts of tubes and dripping bags and beeping machines.

"Hi, Nonna," I say, taking her hand. It feels so small.

She smiles up at me. "Jacky. My angel. Make me laugh."

I want to say, *Sorry, Nonna, I don't feel all that funny right now.*

But I don't. "Sure, Nonna."

And I tell her the one joke that always makes her laugh, no matter how often I tell it to her. "Well, I have some sad news, Nonna...."

"Good," she says, because she recognizes the setup.

"There's been a great loss in the entertainment world."

"*Si?*" She's smiling because she knows what's coming next.

"Yes, Nonna. The man who wrote the 'Hokey Pokey' song is dead. But what was really sad was his funeral. They had trouble keeping his body in the casket. They put his left leg in, they put his left leg out and...well, you know the rest."

Nonna is laughing so hard, I'm afraid the machines are going to sound their alarms.

And once again, I realize that sometimes, being Jacky Ha-Ha can be a good thing.

The rest of my family comes in while Nonna's still laughing. Meredith Crawford is with them. Guess she got a Get Out of School Free card, too. Because Mrs. Turner knows Meredith is my best friend. Or was.

Meredith reaches over and takes my hand. "I'm here for you, Jacky," she says.

"Thanks," I say. "How's Bill?"

"Fine. Said that Cherry Mustard Pickle Pepper Slurpee's going to be a huge hit."

Nonna laughs when she hears that. Me too.

This is good stuff. And Meredith's a good friend. The best.

CHAPTER 45

Later that night, when Nonna is resting comfortably at the hospital and we're all supposed to be in bed at home, I crawl out my window.

I figure it's time to climb to the top of the Ferris wheel again. I need to make another solemn vow. One I'm actually going to keep. I'm sending my little devil packing with a one-way ticket.

Everything's easier the second time you do it. I monkey-bar my way up to the top in record time.

But the winds whipping off the ocean are much colder in the middle of October than they were on the last day of summer. I'm shivering, searching for the moon or a shooting star or a glimpse of my future, but

the sky is full of nothing but dark, heavy-bottomed clouds.

I guess it's an omen, telling me I won't get a second chance to promise heaven that I'm going to try harder to be a better person.

Because all of a sudden, there are lights all over the place.

A five-billion-watt spotlight is shining up at me. I'm half blinded, but I can see all sorts of swirling red flashers down below.

Somebody called the cops.

And the fire department. I see their truck. The one with the expandable ladder on top.

Not knowing what to do, I wave. "Hi, guys. Guess what? I can see my house from here."

"Stay where you are!" says a very serious voice through a megaphone. "Do not move!"

Pretty soon, everybody who lives anywhere near the boardwalk is coming out of their homes in their slippers, bathrobes, and parkas-over-pajamas to stare up at the Jacky Ha-Ha Show, now playing for one night only, on top of the Ferris wheel in Seaside Heights, New Jersey.

I think about doing a quick improv. Something about the world's largest hamster wheel. But I see my sisters.

Riley and Hannah are sobbing hysterically.

"Don't jump, Jacky!" cries Hannah. "You have too much to live for. There's fudge in the fridge!"

Jump? How crazy do they think I am?

Okay. I see their point. What would I think if one of my sisters, say Emma, climbed up to the top of the Parachute Drop or something?

Speaking of Emma, I can see her down below, too. Emma is not crying. Emma is scowling.

BEWARE
of the THUNDERBOLTS
Coming out of her eyes

And, finally, here comes Dad.

With Jenny Cornwall, of course. He's shaking his head. So is she. It's nice how they do everything together now.

"Stay where you are, Jacky!" my dad hollers.

"Stay there!" shouts the prettiest girl on the beach.

"Don't climb down," says the police officer with the megaphone.

That is so dumb. I could climb down in my sleep.

But when I budge, they all start shouting, "Don't!"

"We told you to stay still!" screams Dad.

"So stay still," adds Jenny. Great, not only did she steal Dad, now she's repeating everything he says. That's not annoying at *all*.

So I don't move a muscle and wait for the fire truck to slowly (very slowly) send up its ladder. When I go to climb down it, I hear another chorus of "Don't!"

I have to wait for a firefighter to come up and get me like I'm some kind of kitty cat stuck in a tree.

"Take my hand," the firefighter says when he reaches the top rung.

I do as I'm told.

I feel like such a baby.

But I feel even worse when we make it down the ladder to the ground.

Because that's where my dad is waiting.

CHAPTER 46

H ow could you do something so dangerous?" my father asks.

Everybody in the crowd wants to hear my response.

"It's actually p-p-pretty easy," I say.

I don't think I was really supposed to answer him. I think it was one of those rhetorical-type questions. Because now my dad lectures me something fierce.

"Of all the dumb things you have ever done, young lady, this is the dumbest, the most irresponsible, the most dangerous..."

I get many more mosts. When Dad needs to catch his breath, Jenny Cornwall jumps in.

"You're lucky I'm not a cop anymore," she says. "Otherwise, I'd be arresting you. Trespassing, reckless endangerment, disorderly conduct..."

While she lectures me, I see the local cops scratching their heads, wondering if they should arrest me for all that stuff, too. One of the police officers goes up to my dad and says, "You want we should run her over to the hospital for a psychiatric evaluation, Mac?"

"That won't be necessary," he says. "I'll give her one of those at home."

He doesn't need to, because when we walk into the bungalow, all my sisters tell me how crazy I am. Except Emma. She just crosses her arms over her chest and shakes her head. I am such a major disappointment.

But the lectures don't end there.

Mom calls. That's right—all the way from Saudi Arabia. I hope AT&T gives the marines a discount on their long-distance charges, because this has to be the longest-distance phone call ever made to our house.

"How could you do something so irresponsible?" Mom asks. "You're smarter than that, Jacky. Much smarter."

I don't give her the kind of wisecracking answer I gave Dad. I just tell her I'm sorry.

I'm biting my tongue.

Because there's something else Mom should worry about back here at home. A pretty girl in a bathing suit named Jenny Cornwall. The former police officer who should be charged with reckless endangerment of an entire family, home-wrecking, and first-degree husband poaching.

When my long-distance lecture is over, Mom tells me to give the phone back to my father.

"Go to your room, young lady," Dad says as he practically rips the receiver out of my hand.

"This is all your fault," I say to him, narrowing my eyes something fierce.

"Go. To. Your. *Room.*"

I run off to bed, certain that Mom and Dad are plotting my punishment. I won't be surprised if I'm shipped to some kind of military academy. One where they don't have a Ferris wheel or even a water tower for me to climb.

My whole world feels...I don't know how to describe it.

Upside down?

Like it's crashing to earth?

Like walls are closing in on me and crushing me?
Like all of the above?

I cry myself to sleep again. And this time, my big sister isn't there to cry with me.

CHAPTER 47

The next morning, while Riley and I are packing our lunches in the kitchen, Dad comes in to lay down the law.

"You are grounded, Jacqueline," he says. "For the rest of the school year. You will go to school in the morning and come straight home in the afternoon. You will not attend play practice."

"B-b-but…" I try to say.

Dad ignores me. "I repeat: You will not go to play practice. I will call your teacher, Ms. O'Mara, and tell her she needs to replace you in the show."

"It opens next w-w-weekend," I mutter.

"Maybe you should've thought about that before

you climbed the Ferris wheel. And I don't want you participating in this speech contest, either."

"That was Mrs. Turner's idea," says Riley, my trusty sidekick.

"Fine. I'll talk to her, too. I have friends at the American Legion. I don't want you publicly embarrassing this family again."

He means my stutter. I know it.

"Now go to school. Both of you."

Riley and I slump out the front door.

"I'm so sorry," says Riley when we're two blocks away from home.

"It's okay," I say quickly, because I see a New Jersey Transit bus lumbering down the main road. "Can you lend me some money?"

"What for?"

"I need to go see Sydney."

"In Princeton?"

"Yes."

"But what about school? And Dad?"

I try to act like a tough guy. "What's he gonna do? Double-ground me? Hurry. This is the last bus to Newark...."

Riley, my biggest fan, finally gives me all her cash. Fortunately, I have some of my Atlantic City boardwalk money left, too. So I run like a madwoman for the bus. It's heading to Penn Station in Newark, where I can catch a train to Princeton. If I don't have enough for a ticket, maybe I can perform a few improvs at the Newark train station.

That's right. I'm skipping school again. I just can't face seeing all my friends and Ms. O'Mara. I've totally let them down. My stunt on the Ferris wheel means they're stuck without a Snoopy—with very little time to find a replacement.

It takes more than four hours to travel by bus and rail from Seaside Heights to Princeton. After watching evergreen trees roll by on the Garden State Parkway for maybe thirty minutes, I decide to practice my speech. The one Dad doesn't want me to make, which makes me want to make it even more.

I'll show him, says the gutsy little voice in my head.

By the way, the gutsy voice has completely shoved the evil little devil off my shoulder. There will be no more pranks. Not until *after* I win the speech tournament and show my father what I can do.

When I reach Princeton and find my sister in her dorm room, I finally hear some good news: Sydney's doing really well.

Jacky Ha-Ha, on the other hand, is not.

CHAPTER 48

I unload everything on my big sister.

I tell her about my stupid stunt on top of the Ferris wheel.

How Mom called just to yell at me, long distance.

How Dad says I can't be in *Charlie Brown* or make the speech that I didn't want to make but now want to...almost as much as I now want to still play Snoopy.

I even tell Sydney my suspicions about Dad and Jenny C.

And Sydney listens. She listens really well. Over dinner (more pizza) and late into the evening. I just keep unloading everything I've kept bottled up inside for way too long. I'm like a hot two-liter bottle of soda somebody shook up before they unscrewed the cap. I keep gushing and spewing for hours.

Now *that* was a good shrink session.

I end up spending the night with Sydney in her dorm.

"You should ask Dad what's going on," she suggests. "It's probably something extremely boring."

"I'll think about it."

Early in the morning, one of her good friends (a guy named Jim) gives me a ride home to Seaside Heights. When we pull into our driveway, Dad is on the front porch.
Fuming.

"Okay," says Nice Guy Jim when he sees my seething dad. "Gotta go. Chem class." Guess he doesn't realize it's a Saturday. He squeals wheels out of the driveway.

I walk over to the porch. Dad scowls at me.

"At least your older sister had the decency to call and tell me where you were," he says.

I drop my eyes. "I n-n-needed somebody t-t-to t-t-talk to."

He shakes his head. "Poor judgment, Jacky."

And, finally, I've had enough. I basically explode.

"Poor judgment? What about you and Jenny C-C-Cornwall, the p-p-prettiest girl on the beach? How's that for poor judgment? Running around with h-h-her while Mom's off in Saudi Arabia? What I d-d-did on the Ferris wheel might've been d-d-dumb, but it wasn't h-h-horrible. What you're doing to Mom is worse than h-h-horrible. It's d-d-despicable."

"You have to trust that I know what's best for this family," Dad says through clenched teeth. "There's a lot you don't know—"

"Because you're n-n-never around to t-tell us!"

He ignores me and goes on. "—and I don't want to talk about it right now. I don't have to explain myself to you, Jacky, but you're wrong about Jenny. End of conversation."

Just hearing him say "Jenny" makes my blood boil. "N-n-no, it's not! I've *s-s-s-seen* you with her at night and I know you're not l-l-l-lifeguarding!"

His jaw joint starts popping in and out under his cheeks. "Get your butt inside, *now*" is all he can say.

So it must be true. He really is dating Jenny Cornwall while Mom is off serving her country.

I bite my lower lip as I run inside and slam the door. But it doesn't help.

I cry my eyes out for most of the weekend.

CHAPTER 49

On Monday, I slog my way through my classes.

I spend the whole day trapped inside a depressingly numb fog that's thicker than clam chowder. After the final bell, I'm trudging toward the exit so I can drag myself home, when I see my sister Riley blocking the door.

She's not alone.

Ms. O'Mara is blocking it with her.

"And where do you think you're going, young lady?" says Ms. O'Mara, propping her hands on her hips.

"Home," I say glumly. "My dad won't let me be in the show anymore. It's why I missed rehearsal Friday...."

"So I heard. Your sister told me about your father's new edict. I also had the pleasure of speaking with him on the phone earlier today."

"Dad called Mrs. Turner, too," reports Riley. "Said you couldn't do the play *or* the speech contest."

"However," says Ms. O'Mara, "I told your father that what he proposed was unacceptable."

I shake my head to make sure I heard that correctly. "You t-t-told my dad no?"

"Of course I did. Let's not forget our original agreement, Jacky. You were trading play practices for detentions. By my count, you still have nine left to serve."

"Ten," says Riley. "I've kind of been keeping track."

"As any good sister would," says Ms. O'Mara. "You should go home now, Riley. Tell your father that Jacky is with me. Serving her detentions."

"Okay," says Riley. "See you at home, Jacky."

"Ask Emma to save me a slice for dinner, okay?"

Somehow, I know Dad will be "working late" again so it'll be another plain cheese pizza night at the Hart house.

Riley heads out the door.

"So, Jacky, where do you want to serve your time?" asks Ms. O'Mara when Riley's gone.

"Excuse me?"

"Detention hall or onstage?"

"I have a choice?"

"Of course you do. That's the neat thing about life. You always have a choice. What you do, who you become, all of it is, ultimately, up to you, Jacky—not your father, not your mother, not me."

"But if I choose to stay in the play, what'll I tell my dad?"

"I'm not exactly sure," says Ms. O'Mara. "But we'll think of something. We'll improvise."

"For now," says Ms. O'Mara, "so you're not lying to your father, we'll just tell the rest of the cast that they're officially serving detentions, too. One for every rehearsal."

"Can they save them up and cash them in?" I ask. "I mean, if they ever get into trouble. Not that any of them ever will."

"You're right," says Ms. O'Mara. "In fact, I don't think a single member of the all-star cast of *You're a Good Man, Charlie Brown* will ever do anything even remotely ridiculous enough to earn another detention. They probably won't climb any more Ferris wheels, either. What do you think?"

"I think you're right. I think they're all done making stupid choices. Some even made solemn vows about it that they're going to start keeping."

"What about the oratorical contest, Jacky? In or out?"

"My dad doesn't want me doing it."

"What do *you* want to do?"

"Well, a couple of days ago, all I wanted to do was ditch the speech."

"I'm more interested in today, Jacky."

"I want to do it. Almost as much as I want to play Snoopy."

"Good. You should. People need to hear what you have to say."

"B-b-but what about my stutter? I think half the reason D-D-Dad wants me out of the c-c-competition is because I'd embarrass him in f-f-front of his f-f-friends."

"You and I just need to do a little extra work," says Ms. O'Mara. "We can tinker with your 'fight or flight' reaction. Practice your pacing. You have study hall fourth period, correct?"

"Yes."

"Good. That's my free period, too. Here's a pass. Come see me tomorrow. We only have three days."

"Three days? For what?"

"Before the contest at the American Legion lodge, you have to give your speech *here*. Well, not here in the hallway...here at school. Probably the auditorium. Maybe the gym. The auditorium can't hold the whole school."

"I h-h-have to g-g-give my sp-sp-speech to the wh-wh-whole school?" Even my stutter is stuttering now.

"Of course you do; they all need to hear it. Now come on, we're late for rehearsal—I mean detention."

CHAPTER 50

That night, on our last dog walk of the day, I give Sandfleas my prepared speech for the oratorical contest.

I think she likes it. She's wagging her tail a lot. So it's either my speech, or this stretch of the sidewalk smells like pork chops.

When the walk is done and Sandfleas has had her treats, I prepare to read my speech out loud for my sisters. I'm terrified, of course, but I only have a few more days to polish and memorize my talk.

Everybody gathers in the living room.

First, I warm my audience up with a joke. "You

know, when Mrs. T-T-Turner invited me to p-p-participate in this sp-sp-speech contest, I wanted to tell her that asking me to sp-sp-speak is like watching a dog walk on its hind legs. Even if it's not d-d-done well, you're amazed it can be done at all."

They laugh. They even think my stutter is just my setup for the joke. Just like I hoped they would.

"B-b-but what I want to talk about is so important, I c-c-can't let anything keep me silent...."

It's amazing how fast a three-to-five-minute speech can fly by. I have to make certain every single word packs a wallop and, at the same time, is easier for me to say out loud than *wallop*.

"That is so good!" gushes Hannah.

"I wish one of my boyfriends would talk like that about me," says Sophia.

"I'd give it a nine," says Emma. "For a ten, you need to stand up straighter."

"I loved it," says Riley.

"Me too," says Victoria. "Couldn't have said it better myself." That, of course, is the highest compliment a Hart girl can receive from Sister Know-It-All.

"You guys can't tell Dad I'm doing this," I say. "Okay?"

"Why not?" asks Emma.

"Because I said so," Sophia says in her sternest oldest-sister-still-living-at-home voice.

Emma nods. "Oh. Okay."

"When's the contest?" asks Hannah.

"The American Legion contest is still a couple of weeks away. But I have to give my speech to the whole school this Thursday."

"What?" says Riley. "You only have three more days. Aren't you freaking out?"

"A little," I say with a nervous laugh. "Okay—a lot. Ms. O'Mara is going to help me work on some t-t-technical stuff."

"Is she going to make you do tongue twisters to warm up?" asks Hannah.

"I hope not."

My sisters start a round robin of their favorite, funny tongue twisters. Everything from "Betty Botter bought some bitter butter" to "If two witches were watching two watches, which witch would watch which watch?"

I elect not to join in.

But I'm laughing hysterically. So is everybody else.

In fact, we're all laughing so loudly, we almost don't hear the phone ring.

Sophia snatches up the receiver. "Hello?" she giggles into the phone.

Then she holds up her hand. Her face freezes into a frown. She signals us all to quiet down.

Sophia says "Thank you" to whoever is on the other end of the call.

And then she starts crying.

"What's wrong?" I ask.

"That was the hospital. It's Nonna. She's gone."

"Where'd she go?" asks Emma.

I gently place both hands on my little sister's shoulders. "That means she passed away, Emma. Right, Sophia?"

All Sophia can do is nod.

"Nonna is dead?" asks Riley.

Sophia keeps nodding.

All of us sink down on whatever chair or sofa is closest.

There's no more laughter in the Hart house. I wonder if there ever will be again.

"We need to tell Mom," says Hannah, who thinks with her heart more than the rest of us. "We've all lost a grandmother, but she just lost her mom."

"How do we call her?" I say.

"Dad will know," says Sophia.

And so we wait for him to come home. For two— no, three—long, quiet hours. My sisters and I spend the whole time sobbing.

When Dad finally does come through the front door, he gives us his usual greeting.

"Good evening, girls. What'd I miss?"

Everything is what I want to say.

But I can't. I'm too busy crying.

CHAPTER 51

My whole world becomes one long, sluggish dream. Everything is murky. We're all moving around in a slow-motion daze. I want to hop on Le Bike, pedal over to Nonna's rest home, and tell her favorite joke. I want to do an encore performance of *You're a Good Man, Charlie Brown* for her and her friends in the parlor.

I want to hear her laugh again so badly.

But I never will.

My grandmother had a rare gift. She could always make me feel good about who I am. All she had to do was turn to a friend and say proudly, "That's my

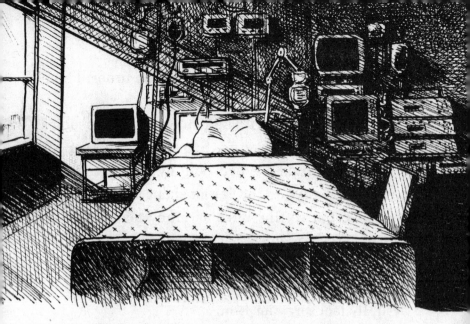

Jacky." And then she'd always brag a little: "When she's a famous star, I can say I've known her since she was so small, I could hold her in my arms."

But she never got to see me be famous, which I'll always regret.

In the days after Nonna passes, Dad is actually home more than he has been since school started. Unfortunately, he's dealing with a lot of what they call logistics. In other words, funeral details.

For instance, since Mom isn't home, he's the one who has to rummage through Nonna's closet and decide what dress she's going to wear to her own burial. After that, he has to go to the funeral home and pick out a coffin.

If you ask me, coffin salesmen are just used car salesmen in darker suits. Sure, they whisper and keep their hands clasped politely in front of their pants while guys on the car lot shout and slap you on the back, but coffins have as many features to sell as cars. Wood or steel? Satin cushions? Embroidered lid? Brass or chrome handles?

Poor Dad. For the first time in a long while, I actually feel sorry for him.

☆ ☆ ☆

At school, Ms. O'Mara is, of course, totally sympathetic.

"Will your mother make it home in time for the funeral?" she asks.

"We hope so," I say slowly. "But it takes almost twelve hours to fly from Saudi Arabia to Newark. And she has to ask the marines to grant her leave, which, of course, they'll do because Nonna was her mom. We just don't know how fast the paperwork will move through the system...."

The whole time I'm spilling out my heart, taking

as much time as I need to tell Ms. O'Mara everything, I don't stutter.

Ms. O'Mara notices it before I do.

"Stuttering," she tells me, "happens when we try to squeeze out words faster than our mouth can handle them."

That's me.

My mind always seems to race ahead of my mouth. My brain is scripting the next "bit" while I'm delivering the first "bit," because when you live for audience approval, there is nothing worse than what radio disc jockeys call dead air. I hate the sound of silence.

Ms. O'Mara and I talk about the body's built-in, adrenaline-charged "fight or flight" response. As in, "Do I stay here and slay this dinosaur, or do I run away and hope it doesn't chomp my butt?"

"Making a speech," says Ms. O'Mara, "triggers

the same kind of adrenalized reaction. How can I stand in front of these people and talk when I really feel like running away? When your adrenaline starts pumping, you feel panicked. You'll want to talk fast and finish as quickly as you can. That's when you need to take a deep breath and give yourself permission to take up your audience's time. As much time as you need."

It's actually good for me to spend my study hall period talking about stuttering and panic attacks and public speaking. It takes me out of Funeral World, if only for an hour. While we work on my speech, I don't worry about Mom missing her flight home, Dad ordering the wrong flowers, or Emma telling the catering company that all we want at the reception after the funeral is plain cheese pizza.

When our time together is almost over, Ms. O'Mara asks me the big question we've both been avoiding: "Do you still want to do this thing, Jacky? Do you still want to make your speech?"

I think about it.

About how much I want people to hear what I've written.

Then Ms. O'Mara drops her next bombshell. "How about *Charlie Brown*? Dress rehearsal is Friday. Opening night is Saturday. If we make the switch today, Colleen could do Snoopy. She'd have to be on book and we'd cut some of your songs, but we'd be okay."

I think about Nonna. In her rest home. In her hospital bed.

"Yes," I tell Ms. O'Mara. "I still want to do both. The speech and the show. I'll make it work. Somehow."

"Yes," says Ms. O'Mara. "We will."

After that, we actually hug. Ms. O'Mara takes my mother's place and whispers softly, "Everything is going to be all right, Jacky. You'll see."

I nod.

I know I'm making the right choice.

But what I don't know is how I'm going to tell my father.

CHAPTER 52

Talk about your "fight or flight" situation.

The instant I step through the front door after play practice (also known as detention), guess who's just about to step out?

You got it. Dad.

He's standing in the foyer, toting this small leather briefcase I've never seen before. Then, behind me, I hear a car crunch across the seashells at the edge of our driveway.

It's that hot little red ragtop again. Jenny Cornwall's convertible.

So, I want to shout, *I see you packed a suitcase.*

Are you and Jenny going someplace special? Want to squeeze in one more romantic rendezvous before Mom comes home?

Of course, I don't say any of that. But the mere thought of saying it actually gives me the courage to say, "Dad, there's something I have to tell you."

"Can it wait, Jacky? I'm in a hurry."

"Fine. I'll make this short. I'm giving my American Legion sp-sp-speech at school this Thursday."

"What?"

"And then, on S-S-Saturday, I'll be appearing in the opening-night performance of *You're a Good Man, Charlie Brown*."

"Your grandmother's funeral is Saturday, Jacky."

"Saturday night?"

"No, but that's irrelevant. You're grounded. And as part of your punishment for climbing the Ferris wheel, I specifically told you that you could not appear in the school play or participate in the speech contest."

"Well," I say, summoning up every ounce of courage I can muster, "you made a mistake."

"Excuse me?"

"Okay, maybe not so much a mistake as a bad

judgment call—like me being dumb enough to climb a Ferris wheel." (I leave out the part about doing it twice.)

Dad's staring at me like I'm a visitor from some other planet.

I keep going.

"We all make mistakes, Dad, because, unfortunately, life doesn't come with an instruction manual. Besides, I'm not telling you I've decided to become a juvenile delinquent. I'm saying I want to give a speech about the duties of citizenship and then pretend to be a dog from the Sunday funnies."

"We'll discuss this later, Jacky."

"No, Dad. No more discussion. I'm doing it."

Jenny Cornwall beeps her horn. Guess she doesn't like her dates keeping her waiting.

"Just a second," Dad calls to her.

Jenny Cornwall shakes her head as if to say, "You have six other daughters, Mac. Why are you wasting your time on *that one?*"

"This is a bad week for this kind of nonsense."

"It's not nonsense, Dad. In fact, it's the opposite of nonsense. It's a sign of intelligence in my otherwise completely screwy universe. Besides, Nonna would want me to do the show."

"Really? And how could you possibly know that?"

"Because it's what she always told me to do!" Yes, I raised my voice. My "fight" adrenaline was kicking in big-time. "'Make me laugh, Jacky. *Make me laugh!*' Those were practically her dying words to me...."

Of course I'm shuddering and blubbering while talking about death and how funny I plan on being.

Dad makes a move, like he wants to hug me. The way he used to hug me when I was very little and the waves crashing against the shore used to scare me.

But the prettiest girl on the beach toots her horn again.

Dad has this sad look in his eye. Like it's fight or flight time for him, too.

And he's all out of fight.

"Okay, Jacky. Make your speech. Do the play. Make your Nonna laugh. I guess we could all use a laugh this week."

Then he dashes down the front steps with his leather satchel, hops into the front seat of Jenny Cornwall's hot little car, and speeds off to wherever it is they go together to try to forget about me.

CHAPTER 53

The next couple of afternoons are eaten up by *Charlie Brown* tech rehearsals and costume fittings.

That means we're working on light cues and set changes and seeing how silly I can look in a face-framing wimple with floppy beagle ears.

Mr. Brimer needs to work through musical cues with his small pit orchestra. That's what they call the group of musicians on piano, flute, drums, and bass who'll be accompanying us while we sing.

Pit orchestra has nothing to do with peaches, cherries, and other fruit with stones for seeds. Or body odor issues.

"Everybody take five" is a common refrain from Ms. O'Mara as Colleen climbs an extension ladder to refocus a light or Mr. Brimer and the pit kids pencil in notes on their sheet music.

So for those of us in the cast, it's hurry up and wait time.

Since there's so much downtime, I'm able to practice my speech backstage and in the dressing rooms. I give my Duties of Citizenship talk to Bill, Dan, Meredith, Jeff, and Beth so many times, I think they

Four paws and twenty dog biscuits ago...

could give it for me on Thursday.

Before I know it, it's Thursday.

I'm so nervous I nearly wipe out on Le Bike on my ride to school. One probably shouldn't practice one's oratorical skills, with accompanying hand gestures, while pedaling.

The morning announcements, delivered over the PA system by Mrs. Turner, stir up the butterflies that have been cocooning in my stomach ever since the assistant principal first told me her nutty idea about Jacky Ha-Ha entering a p-p-public speaking competition.

"And remember," says Mrs. Turner's voice over the speaker, "today's the Big Day. Please join THE ENTIRE SCHOOL in the gymnasium during final period for the first round of the American Legion Oratorical Contest. Six of our BEST SPEAKERS will compete, ONE-ON-ONE, to see who WILL SURVIVE and represent our school at the local competition and then, after more GLADIATOR-STYLE COMBAT, move on to the state tourney in Trenton, and then, IF THEY'RE STILL ALIVE, the nationals in Washington, DC."

Well, that's what *I* hear.

Meredith, who's in my homeroom, turns to me.

"Wow," she says. "Sounds like you're going to be doing some traveling."

"M-m-maybe," I say. "But f-f-first I have to make it through today."

"Jacky?"

"Yeah."

"Take your time. People will like what you have to say. And we have all the time in the world."

"True," cracks Jeff Cohen. "Because if you rush through your speech and the assembly's over early, they'll make us go back to class. And I have math for my final period, Jacky. Math!"

To ramp up the pressure a few more notches, last night Sydney came home from Princeton (where, of course, she's making straight A's again), saying she "wouldn't miss my little sister's big speech for anything in the world."

In fact, my whole family is planning on coming to the middle school this afternoon to hear me t-t-talk. This morning, before I left home, I saw Dad, standing in his boxer shorts, ironing his navy blue suit. Emma has also selected special attire for my big day. How can I bomb with Madonna in my corner?

CHAPTER 54

It's Thursday afternoon. I'm staring at the clock as it creeps toward two p.m.

The assembly starts at 2:15.

Suddenly, there's a knock at the door. The teacher opens it. Ms. O'Mara is on the other side.

"Come on, Jacky," she says. "It's showtime."

"Good luck!" says Meredith.

"Yeah," says this boy in the third row. "You're gonna n-n-n-need it!"

Yep. It's Bubblebutt, that obnoxious kid from detention hall, who's been making fun of me since kindergarten.

"Remember what we do with critics, Jacky?" asks Ms. O'Mara as we march down the hall toward the gym.

"Yes," I answer. "We ignore them. In fact, I'm ignoring Bubblebutt already."

"You mean what's-his-name."

"Exactly."

Even though the bell hasn't rung for seventh period, a steady line of people is already trickling into the gym. I'm guessing the other speech-givers invited their whole families, too.

Ms. O'Mara reaches for the gym door handle and just sort of stands there, looking at me.

There is a devilish glint in her eyes. She smiles a crooked, goofy grin.

"What?" I say. "What's going on?"

Her whole face lights up as she yanks open the door. "Surprise!"

I have no idea what she's talking about.

Until I step into the gym.

And there she is.

Mom!

I can't believe it.

Mom made it home for Nonna's funeral. In fact, she's early.

Maybe she wanted to come to my funeral, too—also known as making a speech in front of the whole middle school.

Mom looks as if she just hopped off a transport plane and raced here to be with me on my big day—she's dressed in her desert camo uniform and I see her huge duffel bag lying on the gym floor. She throws open her arms and the whole world and all its problems melt away.

We're hugging like crazy. We're both crying a bunch, too. Tears mix with laughter.

"I missed you so much," I say into her shoulder.

"I missed you, too, Jacky. You are my laughing girl. My happiest baby."

She squeezes me tighter.

"I'm so sorry about Nonna," I say.

"Thank you, hon. I'm sorry she can't be here today to hear you speak. I know she would've been so proud."

Before I'm ready to let go, Mom's arms loosen around me.

"Mac?" she says.

"Hey, beautiful."

Dad, looking very dapper in his navy blue suit, rushes across the gym floor, like he's charging across the baseball diamond, trying to steal second base. Mom leaps into his arms. They kiss like crazy.

My six sisters drop their eyes and shake their heads. This Public Display of Affection is a little too, well, public. The class change bell just rang. Middle schoolers are filing into the gym. Kids here know us. Several are giggling and pointing at Mom and Dad, who are still acting like they're seventeen again, floating under the mirror ball, dancing the last slow dance at their high school prom.

Me? I don't mind the PDA.

Hey, Mom's been in a war zone for months. Dad's been home, heartsick, pining for her.

Wait a second. Scratch that.

Let's not forget Jenny Cornwall. Suddenly, I'm not so keen on my parental unit's kissy face display, either.

I clear my throat.

"Careful," I joke, because joking is what I always do to mask what I'm really feeling. "You two keep that up, you could wind up with ten detentions each."

"Well," quips my mother, "at least we'd all be serving them together."

And then, I kid you not, my father actually jumps to my defense. "Jacky hasn't had a detention in, what, six weeks?"

"Something like that," I answer. "I've been working them off—"

"At play practice," says Dad. "She's starring in *You're a Good Man, Charlie Brown*. Opening night is Saturday."

O-kay.

I am now totally confused. Is Dad really proud

of my accomplishments? Or is he trying to buy my silence?

After all, I'm the only one of his seven kids who's directly confronted him about what he's been doing with Jenny Cornwall while Mom's been over in Saudi Arabia.

But then Mom comes over to wish me luck.

She wraps her arms around me and squeezes me tight.

And, once again, the whole world and all my worries melt away.

CHAPTER 55

G ood afternoon, ladies and gentlemen."
Mrs. Jordan, the teacher with the pointedly
precise pronunciation skills and clipped diction—
the one who wasn't too crazy about me being invited
to this speechmaking rodeo—runs the assembly.
You can make out every single vowel and consonant in her sentence as if they were individual countries on a map. (And yes, the idea for my *Saturday
Night Live* character, Priscilla the Prude, was born
during this very same middle school speech tournament.)

Mrs. Jordan goes over the rules of "The Prepared
Oration." How we have to talk about some aspect of

the Constitution, with emphasis on a citizen's duties and obligations to our government. How we can't bring a copy of our written speech to the microphone with us. Then she gets into so many of the nitpicky rules that at least half her audience takes a nap. Hey, it's the middle of the afternoon. In some countries, naps are mandatory at this hour. They call it siesta time.

Finally, she introduces the first contestant. He's wearing a suit and looks like a grown-up.

Oops. Wish I'd thought of that.

I mean, not that I would've borrowed Dad's one blue suit, just that I might've worn something besides my best pair of jeans.

"Our first presenter," says Mrs. Jordan, "is Mr. John Valeri, a ninth grader, who placed second last year at the New Jersey state level of the American Legion Oratorical Contest, where he earned a one-thousand-dollar scholarship."

Wow. When she says it, you can hear both *d*s in *thousand-dollar*.

John Valeri is pretty good. So are the four other contestants coached by Mrs. Jordan. I hear every single one of *their* consonants, too. I also feel sorry for the folks in the front row when Catherine Hendee speaks. The girl uses a lot of *p* words. Each one explodes out of her mouth in a misty puff of spittle.

PEOPLE
PLEDGING
PLENTY PAY
PROMPTLY

"And finally," says Mrs. Jordan, looking over the frames of her glasses like she just spied a water bug skittering across the gym floor, "last but not least, Miss Jacqueline Hart."

I get a thunderous ovation from one section of bleachers. It happens when you have six very boisterous sisters who aren't afraid to clap their hands and whoop like they're at a Giants game.

I take a deep breath.

And tell myself, "Take your time." Own this moment.

Jacky Ha-Ha is on.

"Uh, h-h-h-hi."

I hear a loud "Ha-ha" from the crowd. Bubblebutt and Ringworm.

"I'm Jacky Ha-Ha-Ha-Ha-Hart...."

This is worse than kindergarten. My eyes start to fill as they dart around the auditorium. I see a lot of horrified faces. Jaws are dropping. Whispers float their way up to me. All I want to do is bolt off the stage and out of the school, but I'm frozen.

And then I see Mom.

Her gentle smile reminds me so much of Nonna,

I hear my grandmother's voice in my head: *"Make me laugh, Jacky. Make me laugh."*

A joke.

My speech starts with a joke. I *know* I can tell a joke. Aren't I Jacky Ha-Ha?

I take another deep breath.

CHAPTER 56

When Mrs. T-T-Turner invited me to p-p-participate in this sp-sp-speech contest," I say, nice
and slow, "I wanted to tell her that asking me to
sp-sp-speak is like watching a dog walk on its hind
legs. Even if it's not d-d-done well, you're amazed it
can be done at all."

My audience laughs. I smile.

"When it comes to a citizen's duty to their coun-
try, some citizens have more duties than others.
For instance, I'm proud to say my mother is Staff
Sergeant Sydney Labriolla Hart of the United States
Marine Corps."

I don't dare look at Mom.

When I wrote my speech, I didn't know she'd be in the audience to hear me talk about her. If I see her face, I suspect I might feel the need for speed and flip the stuttering switch to *on*.

So I use another one of Ms. O'Mara's public speaking tricks: I keep my eyeline a couple of inches above my audience's heads.

"My mother is a citizen soldier," I say. "She chose to do a dangerous and, sometimes, deadly job. No one forces her to put on a pair of baggy camouflage pants and a floppy hat with brown cow splotches all over it. But that's what she does, every morning, in one-hundred-and-ten-degree heat.

Why does she decide to get up every day, thousands of miles away from her family? you might be wondering. I'll admit that I wonder that too, sometimes.

It's because it's her duty. She made a solemn vow. How many of us have made solemn vows and then actually lived up to the promises we made? How many of us do it every day, even when it means sand in our shoes, a bad case of helmet hair, and very limited fashion options?"

The audience laughs.

"How many of us would keep our word when keeping it means that other people may want to kill us? And my mother is just one of the thousands of citizen soldiers who all have one very important thing in common. When they joined the military, every single one of them raised their right hand and solemnly swore to support and defend the Constitution of the United States against all enemies, foreign and domestic, so help them God.

"You know, I've spent a lot of Sundays, lately, talking to God. Asking Him, or Her, to help my mother, and all the other mothers and fathers and brothers and sisters who raised their right hands and solemnly swore to do their duty.

All those citizen soldiers who are now in harm's way, standing guard on a wall or huddled in the desert, or soaring across the sky—all of them out there defending our Constitution. These Americans surely know their duty to their country, because they live that duty, every day.

"They also stand as a shining beacon of inspiration, showing us how we can choose to live *our* lives. How we can all choose to serve something bigger than ourselves. Something more important. We can all make the same kind of vow to do our duty, whatever that duty might be.

"Because it is only in so swearing and so doing that those of us living in this wonderful country can secure the blessings of liberty to ourselves and our posterity, which, by the way, means 'our children and all their children.' What Mom has done for me, I hope to someday do for others. Maybe in the marines or the other armed services, or maybe not. But I will listen for my calling, find my duty, and then I will do it, so help me God.

"And each of you, as citizens—I implore each of you to perform your own duties to our country, in whatever way calls to you, big or small."

Now I finally turn to the audience to do the bit I thought I would do to the ceiling.

I find my mother in the bleachers again. She's smiling at me, proudly. I smile back.

"I need to thank you, Mom, for protecting and defending the Constitution of these United States of America so that I, and all my sisters, can fully enjoy our blessings of liberty. And that's a lot of liberty, folks. There's seven of us!

"Thank you."

When I finish, the whole audience—not just my personal cheering section—rises up and gives me a standing ovation.

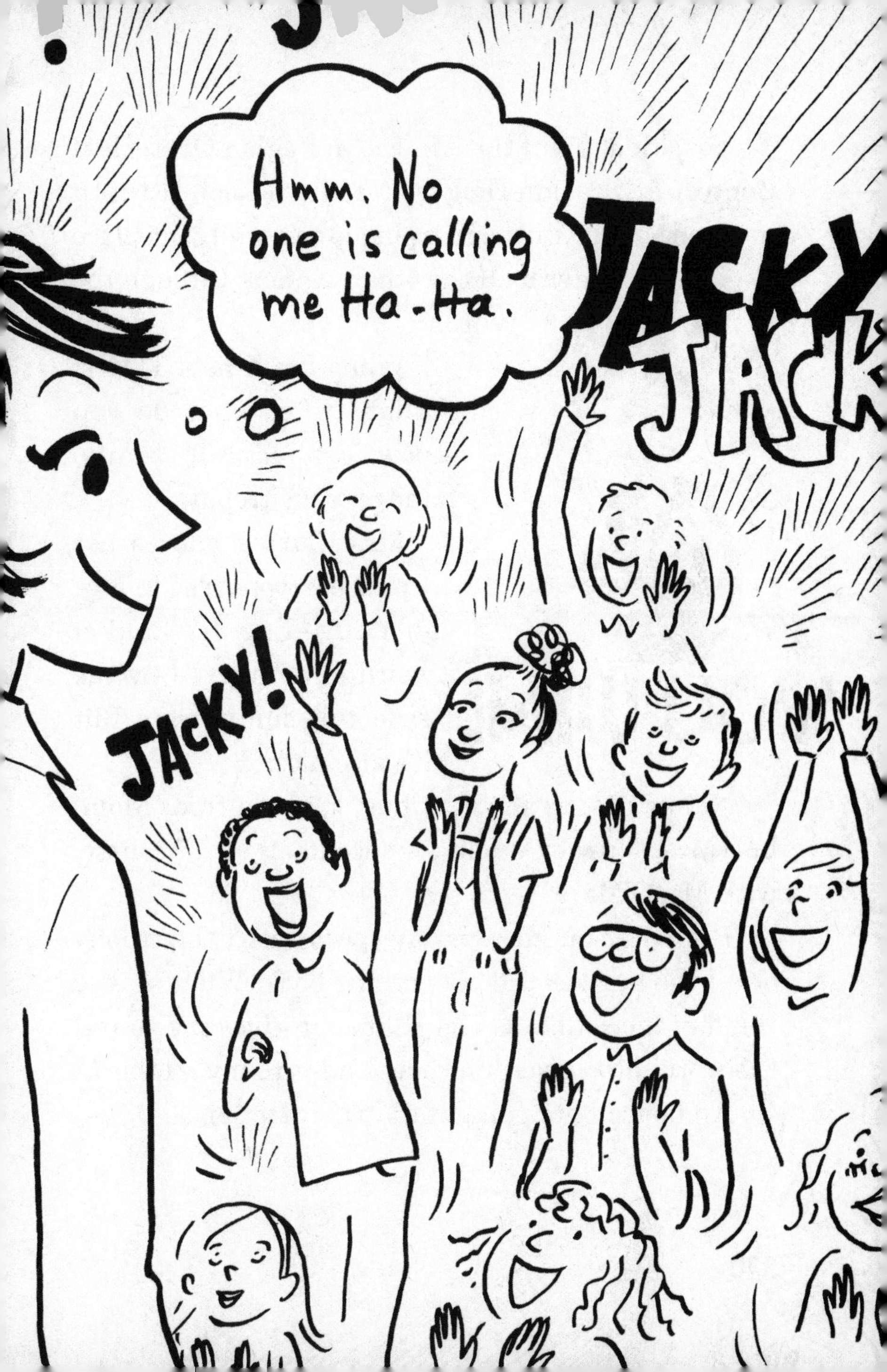
Hmm. No one is calling me Ha-Ha.
JACKY
JACK
JACKY!

Yes, kids, I win the American Legion Oratorical Contest at Seaside Heights Middle School. (I think my name might still be on a plaque on a wall someplace with all the other winners through the years.)

When I'm finished, Mrs. Jordan (who, what do you know, can actually smile) hands me my trophy.

Mrs. Turner shoves her way past everyone else to give me a huge hug. It's kind of weird to be hugged by the school disciplinarian. But it's also nice.

Not as nice as my next hug, the one from Mom, but Mrs. Turner came in second, tied, of course, with Ms. O'Mara.

But what makes the day special isn't the trophy or all the hugs or the pats on the back. What makes the day incredible is the chance it gives me to tell the world how much I love and admire my mother.

And once I got going, I didn't stutter once.

CHAPTER 57

The next day, it's incredible to be waking up with everybody under one roof—even though none of us are happy about the reason for our impromptu family reunion: Nonna's death.

Mom and Dad are handling all the last-minute details, together. (As far as I know, Jenny Cornwall is not being consulted on, say, what shade of lipstick Nonna should wear in her open casket.)

We all head off to school, of course.

Lots of people are still congratulating me about my speech, which, I am relieved to say, is over, done, and finished.

Until, of course, I have to go to the American Legion Hall in a couple of weeks and do it all again, plus be prepared to do that spontaneous speech on one of five topics, too.

But I can't worry about that right now. As Ms. O'Mara reminds me, I have to stay where my feet are.

Today, that means play practice, because it's Friday and *You're a Good Man, Charlie Brown* opens *tomorrow!*

And my mother is going to be in the audience! Not that I'm nervous or anything...I always quiver like a palm tree in a hurricane when I'm calm.

Tonight is our dress rehearsal. That means you try to do the show exactly the way you would do it in front of an audience, but without the audience. It's your last chance to get everything right: acting, music, costumes, lights, sets, props.

We move through our final rehearsal with only a few minor hitches.

Like me falling off the roof of Snoopy's doghouse in the middle of my monologue about how hungry I am.

Fortunately, I somehow worked my acrobatics into the speech. That's the thing about mistakes onstage: Unless you act like you goofed up, people in the audience, who haven't been to any rehearsals or read the script, will never know that you made a mistake. You just have to roll with whatever happens even if what happens is you rolling off the roof.

While I'm taking off my Snoopy makeup in the

dressing room (okay, it's the girls' bathroom), Ms. O'Mara gives me one last pep talk.

"I'm so glad your mother will be able to see you in the show," she says.

"Me too."

"And you know what? I wouldn't be surprised if your grandmother finds a way to be there, too."

I know what she means, but I don't want to get all weepy. So I crack a joke instead. "And Nonna won't even need to buy a ticket."

✧ ☆ ✧

Saturday comes and we all put on our darkest out-fits. Mom's in her dress uniform. Dad's in his one navy blue suit again.

We go to our church, where I, first of all, make sure to thank God for keeping Mom safe.

And then we celebrate the life of the late Isabella Labriolla, beloved mother and grandmother. During the funeral service, each one of us Hart girls takes a turn standing in the pulpit and sharing our fondest memory of Nonna. It's better if we do it instead of Mom. She's a tough soldier, but today she's mostly a bundle of raw emotions and a bucket of tears.

So we work our way down the line.

Sydney, of course, is brilliant. Sophia is emotional. Victoria takes us on a historical tour of Nonna's life. Sweet Hannah says something that none of us can really hear because she's sobbing so much.

And then we reach the middle of the pack.

It's my turn.

"I l-l-loved N-N-Nonna so m-m-much."

I'm a wreck. I can't stop stuttering.

So I stop talking.

I look out at the pews.

My best friend, Meredith Crawford, is sitting in the front row. She silently mouths three words. "Take. Your. Time."

So I take a deep breath and start over.

"Wh-wh-what I loved most about Nonna was how easily she laughed. Even when I had to tell her sad news—like wh-wh-when the man who wrote the 'Hokey Pokey' song died. But what was really sad was his funeral. They had trouble keeping his body in the casket. They put his left leg in, they put his left leg out, and...well, you know the rest."

For the first time ever, Nonna's favorite joke doesn't get a laugh.

Just a chorus of sobs and tears. Including mine.

CHAPTER 58

That Saturday was also the day I first learned the true meaning of the old adage "The show must go on."

No matter how terrible you feel, no matter what tragedies are going on in your personal life, if you are in a play or doing a TV show, the audience is coming to the theater or turning on the TV to be entertained, not to see you bawling buckets of tears because your favorite grandmother passed away.

We get home from the funeral around five o'clock. The curtain goes up on *Charlie Brown* at eight. I'm supposed to be backstage by seven.

In other words, I have two hours to pull myself together and plunk in some Visine so nobody sees how crying turns my eyeballs into a red, murky mess.

While I'm staring at the mirror, I see Dad hanging at the bedroom door.

"Can I come in?" he asks. He's still in his suit. His hands are clasped behind his back.

"I guess."

"That was good, what you said," he tells me. "The speech at the school. And then today. The joke. At the funeral."

Wow. My father is actually nervous talking to me. Talk about the shoe being on the other foot. And, remember, I wear clown-sized shoes.

"These last few weeks have been rough, Jacky," he says. "For all of us. It's good to have your mom home."

I just nod. Because I'm not exactly sure where he's going with all this.

"Anyway," he says, "tonight's your big night. At the funeral, your friend Meredith told me I'm supposed to say *Break a leg*. I'm not exactly sure why. I don't see how you can be Snoopy with a cast on your leg. And I've never seen him in a wheelchair in the comics...."

"*Break a leg* is just a way of saying 'Good luck.'"

"Really?"

I shrug. "What can I tell you? Theater people are strange."

Which, I could've added, is why I blend in so well with them. We're all castaways on that Island of Misfit Toys from the *Rudolph the Red-Nosed Reindeer* TV special they run every year before Christmas.

"Anyway," says my father, clearing his throat, "I got you a little opening-night gift."

He brings his hands out from behind his back and hands me a tin windup toy.

It's a Ferris wheel.

"Thanks," I say. "Looks a lot easier to climb than my last one."

Dad nods. His lips become a tight, thin line. "It's like you said, Jacky, we all make mistakes. Me included. I'll tell you more when the time is right. But being a father doesn't come with an instruction manual, either. I probably yelled more than I should've...."

For half a second, I feel like we're seriously bonding. That we've reached some new level of mutual understanding teetering on the verge of mutual respect.

And then I realize, *Wait a second*. He's just trying to buy my silence with a cheap little Chinese trinket that he probably bought for five bucks in a bargain bin on the boardwalk. His "mistake" was running around town with Jenny Cornwall while Mom was overseas.

His other mistake was thinking I'd ever let him get away with it.

I'm seriously considering decking him when Meredith bursts into the room.

"I am so excited!" she gushes. "I couldn't sit around

my house waiting any longer, so I came over here to sit around and wait with you."

Dad smiles and backs out the door.

"Break a leg, you two," he says.

And when the show's over, I'm thinking, *I'm going to come home and break both of your kneecaps.*

CHAPTER 59

Yes, the show must go on, even when you think your father is a jerk.

My whole family and their assorted friends—including Sophia's boyfriend of the month, the nice preppy, Mike Guadagno—have opening-night tickets for *You're a Good Man, Charlie Brown,* so, once again, I have my own private cheering section.

I'll say this much for Dad: At least he didn't invite Jenny Cornwall to the play. She probably would've worn her Baywatch swimsuit.

The auditorium is packed. I think the entire

middle school came with their parents. I see a lot of younger brothers and sisters, too.

"Okay, guys, huddle up," says Ms. O'Mara when it's five minutes until showtime. We form a circle at center stage, hidden behind the curtain (but we can definitely hear the hubbub and buzz of the crowd on the other side).

"Whatever else is going on in your life," says Ms. O'Mara, "school stuff, boy-girl stuff, family stuff—whatever—I need you to block it out. Those people out there in the audience didn't come here tonight to see *you*. They came to see Charlie Brown and Linus and Lucy and Schroeder and Snoopy and Patty. They came to be magically transported out of whatever is going on in *their* world and into the world of *Peanuts*. That's your job—to take them on that ride. So have fun, give it everything you've got, and know one thing: I have never been prouder of any cast I've ever worked with."

I can't resist cracking wise. "What about all your pals back on Broadway?"

Ms. O'Mara smiles. "They weren't half as amazing as you guys. Okay, everybody, a little warm-up ritual. You, too, Colleen. Mrs. Yen?"

The stage manager and choreographer join our circle.

"Mr. Brimer?"

Our musical director protests. "They need me in the pit...."

Ms. O'Mara will not take no for an answer.

"Come on, Jimmy. You're a big part of this team and we need you here."

"Oh, all right...."

He rolls his eyes and plays along.

"Now," says Ms. O'Mara, "those people out there are giving us two whole hours of their lives when they could be home organizing their stamp collections. So let's do them all a favor and not completely bomb."

We're all cracking up, even Mr. Brimer.

"Put your hand in the center and repeat after me," Ms. O'Mara whispers. "We're not going to bomb!"

"WE'RE NOT GOING TO BOMB!" we whisper loudly as we all snap our hands out of the circle like a bunch of football jocks and get ready to go on.

Mr. Brimer straightens up his tuxedo jacket, then searches for and finally finds the edge of the curtain. He pulls it back and walks out onto the stage.

The audience applauds.

I peek around the velvet drapes and see Mr. Brimer trapped in a white circle of light. He takes a bow and scampers down the steps into the pit.

When he reaches his podium, he adjusts his tux coat one last time and raises his baton.

The band strikes up the overture.

I'm still peeking around the curtain, because there's something odd about the front row. There's one empty seat. Right in the middle. Probably the best seat in the whole auditorium.

It has a RESERVED sign taped to its back.

But whoever the VIP is, hasn't shown up.

And then I realize, *Maybe she has.*

The best seat in the house is Nonna's seat.

Ms. O'Mara did that for me.

CHAPTER 60

Okay, twist my arm.

I'll tell you.

I WAS AMAZING AS SNOOPY!

I don't want to say I stole the show, but, well, the little dog does have some of the best songs and funniest scenes, so, okay, I stole the show.

Meredith was amazing as Lucy. If *The Voice* had been around in 1990, chairs would've been spinning, trust me.

Everybody else was fantastic, too. Even Therese Wiese, the little sixth grader who had a walk-on part as Woodstock, the tiny yellow bird, was hysterical.

When our curtain call finally ended (can you say "standing ovation"?), we called Ms. O'Mara, Mr. Brimer, and Mrs. Yen up onstage and presented them each with a dozen roses.

The flowers were Beth Bennett's idea. She's come a long way since that morning the cast list went up and she went nuclear about not landing the part of Lucy.

I guess we've all come a long way in the weeks we've spent together in our Charlie Brown family.

That's what happens every time you do a show—on stage, on TV, or in the movies. You become this big, complicated family, full of love and jealousy and weirdness and quirks.

But no matter what, you stick together. Because there's nothing like being out there together, creating something none of us could create alone, soaking up the love of strangers you can't even see because the blindingly bright lights turn your unknown admirers into a hazy collection of shadows.

There's a cast party at Ms. O'Mara's apartment after the opening-night performance.

Bill, who was amazing as Charlie Brown, wants me to go.

"I hear she's serving Cherry Mustard Pickle Pepper Slurpees," he says.

That makes me smile, because I know he's really forgiven me for my stupidity at the 7-Eleven. I guess that's another thing backstage families do. Maybe it's what real families need to do, too.

"I'll come to the closing-night party next weekend," I say. "Promise."

"Sure," says Bill. "I understand. How long before your mom has to ship out again?"

"Couple days, I guess. They only gave her a one-week leave."

"So go on," says Bill. "Hurry. Your family's waiting for you."

I head for home.

And pray that Jenny Cornwall's little red convertible isn't parked in our driveway.

CHAPTER 61

We need to celebrate!" Mom says when we pull into our (thankfully empty) driveway.

"Definitely," says Dad.

"You were very good, Jacky," gushes Hannah.

"You were," says Victoria. "But I have a few notes...."

Suddenly, another vehicle pulls in right behind us. Dad glances up into the rearview mirror.

"Perfect timing," he says.

We all tumble out of our minivan and discover a tiny VW Cabriolet (it's like a convertible, only boxier) with a magnetic THREE BROTHERS FROM ITALY PIZZA sign slapped on its door.

We all look at Emma.

"I didn't do it!" she says.

Dad walks over to the pizza guy. "Here you go." He peels off several bills and takes five cardboard pizza boxes.

"Plain cheese, right?" says Emma.

"One," says Dad. "For you and Victoria. Two pepperoni pies for Sydney, Hannah, and Riley. One Hawaiian, with pineapple and ham, for our star, Snoopy, and Sophia. And finally, saving the best for last, one with extra sausage and artichokes."

Mom puts her hands over her heart. "My favorite. You remembered."

☆ ☆ ☆

The next morning, the fun continues. Mom makes everybody pancakes. Dad handles the bacon, sausage, and hot maple syrup.

Since it's Sunday, we all go to church. And, somehow, we all fit in the same pew. I guess this is what they mean about families being close.

My prayers on this particular Sunday are filled with gratitude and thanksgiving.

For Mom's safe return home.

For Nonna's wonderful life.

For Ms. O'Mara putting up with me and putting me in her play.

For Mrs. Turner insisting that I give that speech, because I got to tell the world about my incredible mother and have her hear what I think about her, too. That's a rare opportunity. Kids don't get to say nice things about their parents in public too often.

After church, we all pose for our annual Christmas card photo, even though it's not even Halloween.

We just don't know when we'll all be together again.

Even Sandfleas cooperates and actually looks at the camera instead of licking herself like she usually does when you take her picture.

Our best Family Sunday ever takes a very weird turn, however, around three o'clock.

Dad's napping on the living room sofa, sleeping off all that maple syrup.

Mom taps me on the shoulder.

"Come on, Jacky," she whispers mysteriously. "I want you to go for a ride with me."

"Where?"

"You'll see. Come on. Don't wake your father."

We tiptoe out of the house, climb into the van, and head west. Just the two of us.

We cross the causeway bridge to the mainland and take Route 37 over to a town called Toms River. Yes, the river is named Toms River, too. Maybe the toothpaste guy from Maine used to own property in New Jersey.

Anyway, pretty soon, we're pulling up to a small house. I notice a tricycle with pink handlebar streamers lying sideways in the lawn. There's a football in the rock-lined flowerbed, too.

"So, who lives here?" I ask.

"Friend of the family," says Mom, unbuckling her seat belt. "Come on. I want to introduce you."

We walk up the concrete path and Mom rings the doorbell. A few seconds later, the front door whooshes open.

Mom won't have to make any introductions. I already know the lady.

She knows me, too.

It's Jenny Cornwall. The prettiest girl on the beach.

CHAPTER 62

O kay, girls, brace yourselves.
This is where your humble narrator, your

mom, admits something I know you two will find extremely hard to believe: Sometimes I make mistakes. And sometimes they're huge, gigantic, enormous, elephant-sized mistakes.

This was one of those times.

"Hello, Jacky," says the prettiest girl on the beach.

"Uh, hello," I say. "So, have you, uh, ever met my mom?"

"We've been friends for years," says Mom. "Mind if we come in, Jenny?"

"Not at all."

We head inside, sit down in the kitchen, and, finally, I learn the truth.

Jenny Crawford wasn't "dating" my dad, she was *tutoring* him.

She's a former police officer, remember? Well, it turns out my father is studying to become a cop. And he's doing it for us—his family.

If Dad passes the test and starts earning a police officer's salary, Mom won't need to reenlist with the marines for us to "make ends meet." That would mean she could come home, maybe find a part-time job, and have pancake Sundays with us every Sunday. Forever!

see the
Doughnuts?
PROOF
she used to
be a **COP!**

"Why didn't Dad tell us?" I ask Mrs. Cornwall (yes, she's married and has two little kids—a boy and a girl, or, as I like to refer to them, the football and the tricycle).

"He was afraid," she explains.

"He took this same test seven years ago," says Mom.

"I don't remember that," I say.

"Because you were five, Jacky. Anyway, Mac failed. He was afraid he might fail again. So he made me promise to keep this a big secret."

"Me too," says Jenny.

"But," says Mom, "that was probably a mistake."

I nod. "Dad says adults make 'em, too."

"We do," says Mrs. Cornwall. "Mac didn't want to get everybody's hopes up just to disappoint you guys."

Sounds like somebody I know who didn't want to make a speech or act in a school play because she was afraid she might embarrass her whole family.

That would be me.

"It's why he worked so hard," says Mrs. Cornwall. "Late at night, Saturdays and Sundays. You know your father. He's the straightest arrow I've ever met. No way would he study while he was on the clock in Seaside Heights. He said it wouldn't be right."

"He told *me* it would be stealing," adds Mom.

"And then, when he did become a cop," I say, "he'd have to arrest himself."

Mom and Mrs. Cornwall smile.

Yes, I have found that, sometimes, making a joke can be the best way to ease into an apology.

"I guess I didn't make it any easier for you guys to hit the books," I say. "I'm sorry I acted like such an idiot."

"That's okay, Jacky," says Mrs. Cornwall. "By the way, that night at the Ferris wheel?"

"Yes?"

"Your father was extremely impressed with your climbing ability."

"Really?"

"I think he was sort of proud. But don't you dare tell him I told you that!"

I hold up my right hand and make another solemn vow. "Never. I promise."

We all chuckle a little.

"So," I ask. "Did he make it? Did he pass the test?"

"We don't know yet. They won't post the scores for another two weeks."

"Well, can I at least thank Dad for trying?"

Mrs. Cornwall nods. "I think he'd like that."

Mom pushes back from the table, stands up.

"Thank you, Jenny, for your time today. And for helping Mac."

"It was my honor. Your husband is a very good man."

"I know," says Mom. "Handsome, too. Best-looking boy on the beach."

We head out of Mrs. Cornwall's house and take the long, silent walk to our van.

When we're both buckled in, Mom turns to me. "Okay, Jacky?"

"I'm really, really, *really* sorry."

"I know, hon. But don't tell me. Tell your dad."

CHAPTER 63

So, even though I'm more nervous than I was before I gave my speech or when I made my first entrance in the show, I do just that.

I march into the house and ask everybody to "please step outside for a few minutes so Dad and I can talk. In private."

"What?" moans Sophia. "That cute boy Chad from Rutgers Prep might call!"

Hannah gasps. "What about Mike Guadagno? Don't you break his heart again!"

Then Victoria chimes in. "I'm ready to go over my show notes with you, Jacky."

"Girls?" Mom bellows in her best staff sergeant voice. "Outside. On the double."

Everyone listens. Remember, my mother is a marine. People listen to marines.

Move it, two, three, four, Out the door, two, three, four!

It's just Dad and me in the living room.

Me and the toughest audience I'll ever face.

"Dad?" I say. "I'm sorry. For saying those mean and horrible and nasty things about you and Mrs. Cornwall. I'm sorry for even thinking them."

"I love your mother, Jacky. No matter where she is, no matter how long we're apart...I'll always love her. And I'll always love *you*."

He stops for second, like he's trying not to get choked up. Dads don't like to cry. But I'm already halfway there. When he tells me he'll always love me, I just nod, because I can't even speak.

Then he goes on to say something even harder. "And, Jacky...I shouldn't have let you go on thinking the worst about me and Jenny. I'm sorry. I know I made mistakes when all I was trying to do was be a good father. Some pretty whopping *big* mistakes. But I promise, that doesn't mean I'll ever stop loving you."

"I love you, too, Dad!" I say, all croaky and teary. "More than ever. And thank you."

"For what?"

"For trying so hard. For trying to make everybody else's life better even if it means making your own life miserable."

"My pleasure," he says with a wink. "That's what dads are for."

Have I mentioned that my dad has a wicked sense of humor?

"You know what?" I say.

"What?"

"You and me. We have a lot in common."

"Well, I've never actually climbed a Ferris wheel. Thought about it, but..."

"I mean we've both been working extra hard, trying to make our lives better when it would've been a whole lot easier for either one of us just to call it quits and keep doing what we've always done."

"I guess that's true...."

"So if anybody ever asks me, 'Hey, Jacky, where'd you get all this drive and ambition?' You know what I'll tell them?"

He shakes his head because, I can tell, he's already choking up.

"I'll tell 'em I got it from you! The best-looking boy on the beach and the best dad in the whole world."

At this point, we're both crying.

And, two weeks later, we found out that he passed the test.

That's why your grandfather, as you know, is now the top cop in the whole state of New Jersey.

EPILOGUE

And so we come to the end of the story, which was also the beginning.

Actually, I'm writing this at three in the morning.

After the Oscars ceremony. And the after-party. And the after-party after the after-party. My feet are killing me. Your mother does not wear heels very often or well, ladies.

Your aunt Hannah was there. She and her husband, Mike Guadagno, drove down from San Francisco to be with me.

Now, I know you two stayed up past your bedtime even though I told your grandparents not to let you. Both of them are usually strict police officers (yes, after the war Mom became a cop, too), except when it comes to you two. But I'll let it slide this one time—because your mother, Jacqueline Hart, won the Academy Award for Best Actress in a Motion Picture last night for my "bittersweet portrayal of a down-and-out boardwalk busker in the dramatic comedy *Cracking Up*." I still can't believe it.

I improvised my acceptance speech, of course, but it started off like this:

"Thank you, ladies and gentlemen."

Yes, my diction was very clipped and precise on that line. Every syllable was its own continent. I figured people in the audience would be eager for a little Priscilla the Prude, seeing how it was the most popular character I ever created during my run on *Saturday Night Live*. (Thank you, Mrs. Jordan, wherever you are, and whatever you're overenunciating.)

"First of all, I want to thank the people who first called what I had talent instead of what everybody else called it: trouble. Or ADD. That would be you, Ms. O'Mara. And you, too, Mrs. Turner. Two amazing women from my middle school in Seaside Heights, New Jersey, who refused to give up on me long after I'd already given up on myself. I hope you ladies liked the muffin baskets I sent. If not, I'll mail you the gift receipts.

"I, of course, need to thank our director, my cowriters, our cast and crew. You guys were my family on the set of *Cracking Up* and I love you all. And let's not forget my best friend since forever, Meredith Crawford. Thank you for singing our title song for us…and congratulations on *your* Oscar tonight, too. Now, please, somebody tell me how to stop that melody from getting stuck in my brain!

"Finally, and most importantly, I want to thank my *real* family. My six incredible sisters, who are the best friends any girl could ever wish for, even in a Disney movie. And our mother and father, who taught us that there's always something in the world much more important than ourselves.

"Extra thanks to my husband, Bill Phillips, and, most especially, my two beautiful daughters, Tina and Grace. You're supposed to be in bed, but if you're not, I hope you're proud of your mom. Because I'm definitely proud of you two!"

And then, yes, Jacky Ha-Ha howled at the moon. *AAAAAH-WOOOOOO!*

Loud enough for all the angels in heaven to hear me. I made sure of that.

My name is Jacky Ha-Ha-Ha-Hart,
and a life of fame and fortune
in the bright lights of the theater
is on the horizon...
if I don't embarrass myself first!

It's summertime on the Jersey Shore, and I'm ready for a lazy, hazy, *crazy* fun time, but I need to balance so many things—a summer job, chores at home, and a big role in a Shakespeare production—while still trying to have a blast with my friends. Will I be able to work AND play—or will I figure out that juggling isn't one of my many talents?

Read all about it in

JACKY HA-HA: MY LIFE IS A JOKE

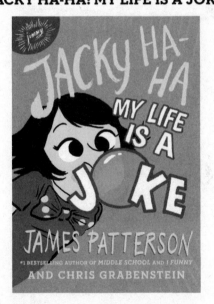

AVAILABLE NOVEMBER 2017

PROLOGUE

Cheerio, Grace! Cheerio, Tina!

No, girls, that's not what I'm suggesting you eat for breakfast. It's the British way of saying "HEY THERE!"

Greetings from LONDON!

Greetings from jolly old England, darling daughters, where I am feeling anything but jolly.

In fact, I might be having a panic attack.

My heart is racing. My palms feel clammy, which is a strange expression, because how can hands feel like clams?

Anyway, I can barely breathe and it's not because somebody just told me what the cute-sounding British dish "bubble and squeak" actually is (leftover vegetables mashed together with cabbage, potatoes, and anything else nobody wanted to eat the day before).

I haven't been this nervous since the time I climbed the Ferris wheel down the shore in Seaside Heights, New Jersey. (The second time. The time my dad caught me.)

I think I am freaking out because I am about to do something I've always wanted to do but am totally terrified of doing.

Yes, that makes about as much sense as a book titled *How to Read* or a waterproof towel.

As you ladies know, your famous mom is over here in London, rehearsing for William Shakespeare's play *As You Like It* at the Globe Theatre. I'm playing Rosalind, one of Shakespeare's funniest, most kick-butt female characters. The new Globe is a re-creation of his famous theater from back in 1599, which, believe it or not, was a year or two before I was born.

Life is good, right?

No. Life right now is *terrifying!*

Sh-Sh-Shakespeare.

Just thinking about playing a part in a comedy by the *Greatest Writer Who Ever Lived* with one of the finest Shakespearean acting companies in the world (or, you know, the *globe*) makes me extremely shaky.

So why is my big opportunity such a huge nightmare?

Because it reminds me of one of the most colossal failures in my whole, entire life.

Most people may know me as the super-cool

Academy Award–winning funny lady and star of *Saturday Night Live,* but that's not who I was one summer when I was about your age.

I was a mess.

And a failure.

The star of a one-woman disaster movie.

So beware: There are hazardous conditions up ahead.

CHAPTER 1

It's the summer of 1991.

Everybody is saying *"Hasta la vista,* baby," and not just in Spanish class, because Ah-nold Schwarzenegger said it in a movie called *Terminator 2: Judgment Day.*

Someday, I'll probably look back on this and LAUGH.

Today, I think I'll just SCREAM in AGONY.

Teenage Mutant Ninja Turtles toys are huge. So is Rollerblade Barbie. What are Rollerblades? Don't worry, you don't need to know. Unless you want to twist your ankle, sprain your butt, and scrape most of the skin off your elbows like I did.

But that's not the big disaster.

In fact, 1991 started out pretty good, especially if you ignored Boyz II Men on the radio. (Yep, they were a thing. And that *II*? It's supposed to be a Roman numeral two, not an eleven.)

In March, Mom came home from Operation Desert Shield, which turned into Operation Desert Storm—a war that, thankfully, only lasted, like, six weeks. Now she's back in charge of running the Hart house.

Did I mention my mom, Big Sydney Hart, was a marine? (She's Big because my sister Little Sydney is named after her.)

"I want to see those dishes shine, girls!" she tells us every night after dinner. "I want this galley to glisten!"

"Aye, aye!" we all say.

"Hoo-ah!" says Mom.

Emma, the youngest, who we used to call the Little Boss, is now the Little Echo. She tells us to do

PUT SOME ELBOW GREASE INTO IT, GIRLS!
PUT SOME GREASE ON YOUR ELBOWS, GIRLS!

whatever Mom just told us to do.

Things are humming along at school, too.

Yours truly hasn't had a detention since I played Snoopy in the fall musical, *You're a Good Man, Charlie Brown*. If you knew me at all, you knew that me not having detention was a miracle!

I also did the spring show—*You Can't Take It with You*. It was a comedy (yay!) and I played Essie Carmichael, a kooky candymaker who dreams of being a ballerina even though she's a terrible dancer.

I was hysterical, girls. Your mother always was (and always will be) a terrible dancer. Terrible can be funny. Especially if it's ballet.

So now it's June, and life is pretty sweet. Mom's home safe and sound. School's almost over. I'm looking forward to a fun-in-the-sun Jersey Shore summer. The beach! The boardwalk! Bill Phillips!

Yes, he still has those crazy-gorgeous hazel eyes and I still have a kind-of, sort-of crush on him. Hey, I'm twelve going on thirteen. It's summer. It happens.

My big plans when school's out?

Goofing off. Lazing around. Hitting the beach. Doing a whole lot of *nothing*.

Unfortunately, Dad and Mom have different plans. *Very* different.

JAMES PATTERSON received the Literarian Award for Outstanding Service to the American Literary Community at the 2015 National Book Awards. He holds the Guinness World Record for the most #1 *New York Times* bestsellers, including *Middle School, I Funny,* and *Jacky Ha-Ha,* and his books have sold more than 350 million copies worldwide. A tireless champion of the power of books and reading, Patterson created a children's book imprint, JIMMY Patterson, whose mission is simple: "We want every kid who finishes a JIMMY Book to say, 'PLEASE GIVE ME ANOTHER BOOK.'" He has donated more than one million books to students and soldiers and funds over four hundred Teacher Education Scholarships at twenty-four colleges and universities. He has also donated millions to independent bookstores and school libraries. Patterson invests proceeds from the sales of JIMMY Patterson Books in pro-reading initiatives.

CHRIS GRABENSTEIN is a *New York Times* best-selling author who has collaborated with James Patterson on the I Funny, Treasure Hunters, and House of Robots series, as well as *Jacky Ha-Ha, Word of Mouse, Pottymouth and Stoopid, Laugh Out Loud,* and *Daniel X: Armageddon.* He lives in New York City.

KERASCOËT is the pen name of Marie Pommepuy and Sébastien Cosset, a couple of French graphic novel authors and illustrators living and working in Paris.